The Just

The Justice Game

The Lady from Rome

PETER TURNBULL

based on an original story and screenplay
by John Brown featuring characters
created by Peter Broughan
with John Brown

Published by BBC Books,
a division of BBC Enterprises Limited,
Woodlands, 80 Wood Lane, London W12 0TT
First published 1990

Cover photographs © John Green show
Denis Lawson as Dominic Rossi
and Anita Zagaria as Francesca Arcalli.

Set in 12/15 Goudy Roman
Typeset by Ace Filmsetting Ltd, Frome, Somerset
Cover printed by Richard Clay Ltd, Norwich
Printed and bound in Great Britain by Richard Clay Ltd, Bungay

They were days that he could not forget, what man could, what man would want to? It was a milestone in his life.

They started with a sombre-faced carabiniere, arriving at the villa . . . no there was no mistake, signor, none I regret, . . . not fifteen kilometres from here . . . no signor, not at the site. Later perhaps at the mortuary . . . No Signor Cristaldi, no, there is no mistake . . . Yes, I'm afraid so, your wife and children . . . Yes, both children . . .

And later, massively attended, and with the media of different nations present, the three coffins being laid side by side. He was in a state of numbness, yet there was also a strange immediacy, smells were stronger, during those few days, colours were louder. . . .

He remembered the old woman approaching him. He had never seen her before and was never to see her again. She was dressed all in black with heavy black shoes; a widow from the town. She walked with a stick, her free hand holding her back just above the kidneys. Frequently she stopped walking and then her mouth would open and shut, open and shut as if she was in great pain, though she didn't make a sound. Eventually she stood in front of him and she said, 'Even if it takes you ten years, signor, even if it takes you twenty, remember that we in Italy have always believed revenge to be a dish best taken cold.'

Chapter 1

THREE MEN LOOKED at their reflections in mirrors. It was an act that most people do each day of their lives. Some might do it lovingly, eagerly, relishing and savouring their own image. Others, perhaps, might do it loathingly and only out of necessity; yet others might do it only by accident, humility not allowing them to seek their own reflection. Three men looked at their reflections in mirrors. They did it for different reasons, but by sheer coincidence, coincidence and nothing more, they glanced at their reflections, or studied their image, or altered their image at precisely the same moment. Yet they were separated, each from the others, by great distance.

The first man was a priest. He was a young man, in his thirties, lean and fit, with dark and angular features. As befitted his calling, and his parish in the mountains, his surroundings were spartan. There was all that was necessary for life in the room in which he stood, his room, and nothing more. He raised his head from the chipped wash-basin while reaching for the towel and, quite by accident, he caught sight of his reflection in the small mirror which hung above the basin on the bare plaster wall. In a moment of indulgence, he allowed his gaze to rest on his image. There had been great changes in his life, changes for the better, and again he noticed a fullness and a warmth in his eyes; something which had not always been there. Once his eyes had been dark and cold. He wiped his face and hands dry and turned away from the mirror and from his past, of which he had been suddenly reminded. He dressed and left the room.

The second man was older than the first, and his surroundings, by comparison, were luxurious. The second man sat at a dressing-table and studied himself in the mirror. He was thickset, with a full, large face. He saw himself as handsome, but another would have seen the steely, cold, hungry glint in his eyes. He leaned to one side and opened the briefcase which rested on the floor beside him. He saw the wig inside the briefcase and beside the wig was the gun, a 9mm automatic, his favoured weapon. The man had a theory about disguises. The trick wasn't to make yourself blend in with the rest of the crowd; it was surprising how often people managed to remember afterwards, under expert questioning, the colour of a dress or the shape of a face. No, the way to do it was to give yourself something in your appearance that made people look away, not want to see out of embarrassment or guilt or shame. In the past, he had used make-up to place a hugely disfiguring strawberry birthmark on his neck and cheek. Only children stared at people afflicted like that. But on this occasion, the wig would suffice. He took the wig and slid it into place on his scalp. Again he studied himself, the wig gave him a thick head of silver hair and altered his appearance completely. He reached again into the briefcase and took out the automatic. He withdrew the ammunition clip from the handle, checked that it was full and slid it back into place. He screwed the silencer, which had lain separately in the briefcase, onto the end of the barrel of the gun. He replaced the silenced weapon in the briefcase, locked the clasp, stood up and silently left the room.

The third man crouched and preened himself before the wing mirror of a car. Like the second man, he too was not displeased with his appearance; he was dark-haired, slim, pleasantly tanned and, like the first man, he was in his thirties. As far as he could see, he looked well in the lightweight suit. He certainly felt well in the garment – it was the latest addition to his wardrobe. He turned from the mirror, walked to the rear of the car and opened the boot from which he took a huge bouquet of flowers.

The three men would meet on the steps of a holy place. One would die there.

*   *   *

Dominic Rossi cradled the flowers as he walked from

the car towards the villa. He surveyed the building as he approached it. It was the first time that he had seen it. It was, he saw, a solid and a substantial property of three floors, white painted with a red-tiled roof. There were tall windows on either side of an imposing doorway and generous stands of cypress trees stood at either side of the building itself. Rossi, taking the image in, half-closing his eyes against the glare from the fierce mid-morning sun, reflected wryly that this was living for some. He glanced around him at the expanse of ground in which the villa stood. It was not, though, he thought, living for others, not for the east-enders of his native Glasgow. This was Italy, basking in the sunlight, a long, long way from damp housing, the poll tax, glue and super lager.

He approached the door, darkly stained and highly polished, and reached for the bell push. As he did so, the door swung silently open; a servant in a dark suit held the door, bowed slightly and ushered Rossi into the cool and calm of the villa's interior. Rossi entered the villa feeling a little uncomfortable and as if he shouldn't be there at all. He followed the servant dutifully and, despite his deeply held convictions of justice for all, was not unimpressed by the marble staircase, the solid old furniture, and the tapestries hanging from the wall. There might well be an unfair share of wealth in this home, he thought, but it was exhibited tastefully and discreetly. It was the sort of wealth that is often called 'old money'.

The servant walked silently across the cool floor and led Rossi to the rear of the villa, onto a terrace. Rossi left the shade of the house and stepped again into the sunlight. The terrace looked out onto a wide expanse of lawn which was dominated by a swimming-pool of huge proportions. The swimming-pool in turn gave way to shrubs and still more cypress trees. A woman with dark hair sat in a chair on the lawn, facing away from the villa and towards the swimming-pool and the trees. Rossi smiled. The servant retreated.

Rossi left the terrace with a lightness and eagerness of step and walked towards the woman. He approached her, holding out the flowers as he did so. The woman turned and faced him. Rossi faltered. She was not the woman he had thought her to be.

'Mr Rossi, I presume?' said the woman.

'For you.' Rossi handed her the flowers.

The woman smiled and accepted the bouquet, but Rossi knew that she had seen the look of surprise on his face when she had turned to him. She was an elegant woman, a young looking late fifties, he thought, a woman who seemed to have not just enjoyed 'old money' all her life, but one who also knew how to use it well and wisely.

'Francesca,' she said, 'will be down in a minute. May I offer you a drink, Mr Rossi?'

'Thank you. . .' Rossi broke off in mid-speech as he noticed Francesca appear on the terrace.

He looked across the lawn at her, struck again by her beauty, just as he had been when he first saw her. She was an elegant, slim woman in her early thirties. She left the terrace and approached Rossi, graciously moving across the lawn, as if she was gliding. She nearly kissed him on the mouth, but at the last moment greeted him as a friend, touching his cheeks instead with her lips. Rossi guessed it was the presence of Signora Arcalli, sitting at the table a few feet away, which had inhibited her. The iron laws of good manners? No, something else. It suddenly came to him that Francesca could keep secrets. The Francesca he had known in Sorrento, mixing business with pleasure, was not necessarily the same Francesca at home. Rossi embraced her delicately and then reached for a single flower from the bouquet. He presented it to Francesca.

'I thought that we had already said goodbye,' Francesca said teasingly as she accepted the flower. 'What time is your plane, anyway?'

'Four thirty,' Rossi replied, holding her gaze. 'Plenty of time for lunch, and more goodbyes.'

Francesca smiled, discreetly and charmingly and, as she did so, Rossi's attention was suddenly drawn towards a small boy, about ten years old, who emerged from the shrubs and ran excitedly and joyfully towards them. Rossi, fluent in Italian, listened somewhat surprised as the boy addressed Francesca as 'Mummy', telling her eagerly about a bird's nest that he had found.

'Dominic,' Francesca turned to Rossi, 'Dominic, this is my son, Sergio. Say hello to Mr Rossi, Sergio.' Sergio and Rossi shook hands, Sergio a little self-consciously and Rossi with amusement.

'Well,' said Rossi, turning again to Francesca, 'what would life be without a few surprises?' He glanced around him at the garden, at the villa. 'It's a nice little place you've got here too.'

He continued to look about him and as he did so he saw a solemn-looking man standing at the edge of the shrubbery, where it bordered onto the lawn. The man remained where he was, making no attempt to join the group which gathered close to where Signora Arcalli was sitting, as if he were not part of the household, and yet he made no attempt to conceal himself.

'Vincenzo,' Signora Arcalli said blandly, as she followed Rossi's gaze, 'he's our . . . nanny.'

'A bodyguard?' Rossi looked at her and raised an eyebrow.

'It is, I'm afraid,' said Signora Arcalli, 'the realities of life in this country.'

Again, Rossi glanced at his surroundings as he nodded in response to Signora Arcalli's explanation but again he thought that the realities of life in Italy for the Arcallis, and for families like the Arcallis, were not necessarily the realities for everyone.

*　　*　　*

The street was crowded, vehicles on the road were bumper to bumper, inching forward, drivers pressing the horns constantly as tempers flared. The pavement was just as crowded with pedestrians bustling and pushing each other. The city of Rome baked under a hot and relentless sun.

The woman struggled with three heavy shopping bags. She felt unwell, the heat was getting to her, the traffic fumes were getting to her. Her legs began to feel weak, her head began to swim. Then, just then, she saw the taxi, sitting at the edge of the pavement, the rear door was even open, invitingly. She made for it, desperately, forging a diagonal path, elbowing her way through the human tide, desperately trying to reach the taxi before another person stole it from her. She reached the vehicle and claimed her prize by flinging the heaviest of her bags onto the far side of the rear seat; she bent down as she got in the car, tugging the bags in behind her, sighing with relief as she sat down. It was only then that she half-noticed the driver was sitting strangely, leaning against the steering wheel with his head on one side. She looked again and began to scream. She didn't hear herself scream but she knew that she was and she became aware of people gathering around the taxi, peering inside, peering, gaping, at her and at the driver. The woman continued to scream because of the driver. She screamed because the driver had a bullet hole in the back of his head and his eyes were open. She screamed because the driver was dead.

*　　*　　*

Rossi swilled the champagne around the glass and wagged his finger playfully across the table at Francesca. At the moment he felt he couldn't care less about flying back to Glasgow and the obligations of employment, but that was the Italian in him and he knew that the Scottish side of him would eventually make its foreign twin pay for any such irresponsibility. Francesca smiled and glanced sideways at the couple at the adjacent table. A waiter passed between the tables and she returned her gaze to Rossi. He was, she thought, a handsome man, a few years older than she was and clearly of Italian ancestry.

'False pretences, I'd call it,' he said smiling, 'I had no idea that you lived in a house like that . . .. mansion might be a better word.'

'It's a villa,' said Francesca. 'And a modest villa at that.'

'Modest!' He was genuinely surprised. 'Is that what you call modest?'

'Oh, there are larger villas,' she said. 'Much larger.

Ours is modest. It has been in our family since it was built by my grandfather when he moved to Rome. Originally my family comes from the south, near Torronto.'

'My father comes from Calabria,' he told her. 'My mother's a Scot from the Western Isles.'

'You didn't want to follow your father into the restaurant business?'

He shook his head. 'I think he was disappointed, but he's pleased that I'm making a success as a lawyer. You must come and visit me in Glasgow. Have dinner at our restaurant.'

'I'd like that, someday.' She smiled.

'And you didn't tell me about . . .' He held his hand out at a child's height. 'You passed yourself off as a humble interior decorator, doing up a hotel.' He grinned. 'I could sue you.'

'I didn't pass myself off as anything. I am a humble interior decorator and, at the moment, I am re-designing the interior of a hotel. Not perhaps the one we were both staying in, but a hotel.'

'You misled the court.'

'Well then, I'm guilty. I admit it.' She looked upwards at the high, richly decorated ceiling and attempted to recall a phrase he had taught her and, remembering, looked at him and said, 'I throw myself on the mercy of the court.' Rossi burst out laughing. There had been a day on the beach when he had started talking about the law, not the abstract principles of jurisprudence but the day-to-day experience of taking people through the intricacies of the system and the thousand-and-one dodges and tricks and manoeuvres of his working life – at least, the way that life used to be – the grammar and vocabulary of the justice game. Francesca had lain in the sun, her skin darkening by the minute in contrast to her pale green bikini, her eyes closed; evidently she'd taken in more than he'd thought.

'That day on the beach wasn't wasted then?'

Francesca's expression became serious. 'It wasn't wasted at all,' she said, 'I learnt so much, I learned about the law, I learnt about you, I learned about me, I learnt about you and I, us.' She extended her hand, reaching out across the table. He laid his hand on hers.

'I didn't know about Sergio,' he said.

'Perhaps I should have told you. I didn't want to scare you away. Some men are funny about other men's children. But I didn't hide him from you. I made no attempt to do that.' Francesca pretended to bow her head in apology and shame. Her shoulder-length hair swung down, concealing for a moment the delicately sharp planes of her face and the wonderful, mesmerising eyes. It wasn't the kind of gesture you would see very often in this restaurant, Rossi thought, a beautiful and expensive setting for beautiful and expensive people. The place had been Signora Arcalli's suggestion and Rossi had guessed at the time that it would demolish the rest of his traveller's cheques. He also suspected that Francesca's mother, back in the mansion with the garden and the pool, was sending him a message. This is how we live – can you afford my daughter?

'Is there a husband?'

She shook her head. 'I never married Sergio's father, well . . . we all make mistakes that we have to live with. Someday perhaps, no someday I will tell you about it. But not now. This is your last day. I don't want to spoil it.'

'Well, in that case,' Rossi raised his glass, 'To beautiful Sorrento and to the Glasgow travel agent who said that was all he could offer me at twenty-four hours' notice.' Francesca raised her glass.

'To Sorrento, and to my decision to take a holiday for a few days.' She sipped her champagne and paused. Then she said, 'You know, I didn't really expect . . .'

'To see me again,' Rossi interrupted her. 'Well, as I told you on the phone, I just thought that I'd take a little detour on the way home.'

'You didn't say why you were taking a small detour.'

'I don't know why I did it,' said Rossi thoughtfully. 'Maybe I can't let things go. What do you think?'

She pursed her lips thoughtfully. 'I,' she said at length, 'I think that holiday romances don't last. Mine never have.'

'That's right,' he said. 'It's realistic. It's important not to be adolescent about this.'

'Absolutely,' she said. 'Let's keep our heads. We both want to see each other again. I'll miss you when you go . . .' The waiter came to their table. Francesca and Rossi leaned back in their chairs as the waiter laid the first course of their meal before them.

'Have you made your big decision?' Francesca changed the subject, speaking as the waiter turned away. 'About your career change, I mean, about becoming, what was that word?'

'An advocate. The English term is barrister.'

'Advocate. That's the word.'

Rossi shrugged.

Francesca persisted. 'I thought that that was the main reason for your holiday. To get away and think about it, solve the problem from a distance, put everything in perspective. That's what you told me.'

'Well,' he said, 'let's say I got distracted.'

She spoke sternly, not letting go. 'You said that you were going to decide after I went home and you had two more days to yourself.'

'You're like a dog with a bone,' he smiled. 'If I tell you that I've made a decision, then can we get back to talking about us?'

21

Francesca raised her eyebrows.

'Okay,' Rossi grinned, 'I've come to a conclusion about my future and the answer is a definite maybe.'

'That's no answer.' She spoke sharply. 'Have you or haven't you?'

'No,' he conceded, 'I haven't.'

*   *   *

In Cocullo, the priest, who had earlier that morning caught sight of his reflection in a small mirror, left his church by the side door. Around the village, the mountains and forest rose in a magnificent splendour which never failed to impress him. He stopped as he left the church, momentarily blinded by the sunlight, and proceeded to cross the square to his motor cycle where it was parked with some others. A group of villagers, his parishioners, stood talking close by. They greeted him as he approached and he stood a while with them, exchanging pleasantries. Presently he left the group.

'Good day, Father,' said one of the villagers, as he began to ride away.

'Good day, Father Pietro,' said another.

*   *   *

A definite maybe. It was not, Rossi reflected as the Clerk spoke to him, a wholly inaccurate answer that he had given to Francesca one week ago. The more he thought about it and the more that he listened to men like this man, the more the answer was still a definite maybe. The future was no clearer than it had been on the day he and Francesca had eaten their last meal together.

'Let me ask you a personal question.' The Clerk was a well-built man, portly, chubby about the face, balding, expensively dressed. He spoke softly with a degree of authority, as he led Rossi through the Advocates' Library, their footsteps softly echoing in the vast, highly vaulted room. Here and there a man sat at a table, either young struggling advocates, thought Rossi, or experienced elders of the profession. Each read from close-printed text books. Some took notes.

'What does your wife have to say about it?'

Rossi thought the question rude, utterly impertinent. Quite irrelevant. He paused before answering and then said, dryly 'I'm not married.' An elderly man looked up as they passed.

'Well,' the Clerk stopped at the door to his office, opened it and gestured Rossi to enter, 'what does your bank manager have to say about it?'

Rossi thought it was another inexcusably personal question; he held his anger in check. He was on strange territory, in more ways than one. He was unsure of his ground and so said, simply, 'I'm not in the habit of turning to him for career advice.'

'To become an advocate, Mr Rossi,' the Clerk closed the door of his office and motioned Rossi to sit in a leather-bound chair in front of the desk, 'a solicitor must first remove his name from the roll. That means that he ceases to practise until such time as he is admitted to the Faculty.' The Clerk sat heavily in his chair behind the desk and looked at Rossi. 'No practice,' he said, and somewhat smugly, thought Rossi. 'No income. Hence my question about your wife and your bank manager. Not being over-personal just, as I understand it is said in some quarters, laying it on the line, just ensuring that you are going into this with your eyes open.'

'Thank you,' Rossi began to change his mind about the man, 'but that's still my problem, not the Faculty's.' Rossi paused and took in his surroundings, a stuffy room, over heavy with books, 'As I understand the system.'

'Ah,' said the Clerk, leaning backwards, 'the system. From what I hear, you are rather against the system, in the larger sense of the word.'

'Oh,' Rossi also leaned back in his chair. 'There's always room for a token revolutionary, isn't there? Even in the Faculty of Advocates.'

The Clerk glared at him.

Outside in the street, Sinclair Murray was waiting for Rossi. Rossi emerged, angered, he and Sinclair Murray fell into step with each other as they walked rapidly away from the Advocates' Library.

'Oh, we hit it off straight away,' said Rossi, in answer the older man's inevitable question. 'Lots in common; my dad owns a restaurant, his owns Aberdeenshire.'

They walked on in silence, Sinclair Murray allowing Rossi to brood. Eventually he asked, as their pace began to slow, 'Speaking of property,' he looked sideways at Rossi, 'how did your roof manage during your holidays? There was a bit of rain while you were away.'

'Don't mention it.' Rossi grimaced. 'I've been back for a week and it seems like I've never been away. I must tell you about this villa I visited. I know I'm a property owner but this was like going back into the Dark Ages, servants, bodyguards, the lot . . .'

Rossi and Sinclair Murray had reached Princes Street, and their pace had slowed to that of a gentlemanly stroll. They walked underneath the Scott Monument, Waverly Gardens to their left, the castle up there on the hill, four lanes of traffic to their right.

'This is what you should have done years ago, Dominic,' Sinclair Murray raised his voice to compete with the drone of an engine as one of Edinburgh's famous white and maroon buses swept past. 'Advocates are like blondes. They have more fun.'

'And gentlemen prefer them.'

'Ha!' Sinclair Murray laughed. 'By the time I've put you through your divilling, you'll be a shining pillar of the establishment,' Sinclair Murray gestured at the impressive Edinburgh cityscape, 'here in the Athens of the North.'

The cannon on the castle ramparts fired. The thump and crack echoed over the city. Both men looked at their watches.

'Really,' said Rossi, his watch had read one minute past one. Good enough. 'It's always struck me as being the Reykjavik of the South.' He paused, and suddenly became more serious. 'I don't know, Alistair, maybe getting into the wig and gown and all that is going to be a bad move for me. I keep remembering Francesca saying . . .'

There was a sudden gleam in Sinclair Murray's eyes. 'And who,' he said, 'may I enquire, is Francesca? Don't look now but your notorious class consciousness is showing.'

Rossi walked on without speaking, but eventually he said, 'May it always.'

*   *   *

It was a small café with tables and chairs of black aluminium tubing and formica surfacing, red and white tiled floor, a fan rotating slowly in the ceiling and an air conditioner rattling noisily. The door was open but flies were excluded by the simple expedient of beads hanging on cords from the top of the door frame. The elderly proprietor stood behind the counter, by the espresso machine. On the wall behind him were posters advertising Gauloises, Beck's Bier and Martini. He glanced up as the strikingly attractive young woman pushed the beads aside and entered the café. He watched as she stood in the doorway, looking about her as if searching for someone. He studied her expression, one of curiosity, he thought, as the woman recognised another customer, a man who had been sitting alone for some time, toying with his coffee but smoking heavily, wearing an expression of worry and concern.

In the doorway, Francesca Arcalli smiled as she recognised Marco. Still smiling, she approached him. He looked up as she approached and he too smiled. He stood, they embraced and kissed, but not as lovers, as old friends. She stood back, still holding him, looking at him. Yes, it was Marco, the same Marco, now in his thirties, but the same Marco, how tense he looks, she thought, how crumpled in that old suit.

'Marco,' she said, as she sat down opposite him, 'it must be ten years . . .'

'You look wonderful,' he interrupted with a nervousness that she thought was utterly unlike the Marco she had known. It was a nervousness that startled her, that told her he was in trouble. It meant that she too had something to fear. It couldn't be that their past was catching up with them, no, not now, not after all these years. Not only was Marco nervous, but he had spoken to her in English. She gave him a puzzled look.

Marco looked around him. 'Just in case,' he said, speaking again in English and tapping his ear with a gesture which had universal meaning. 'Did you take care? Coming here, I mean?'

'No one has followed me,' said Francesca, also speaking in English, in the same hushed secretive tone that Marco had used. She leaned forward. 'Listen Marco, what is all this about?' She forced a smile and tried a poor joke. 'Is your wife having you watched?'

'She's gone,' Marco's tone was deadly serious. 'She left me about a year ago now.'

Francesca made to speak.

'It doesn't matter,' he said, continuing to glance around him.

One customer left the café, another entered. Francesca noticed that Marco watched them both, intently. He was a frightened man. He turned to Francesca and, as he did so, he took a page of a newspaper from the breast pocket of his jacket. It was folded neatly and he slid it across the table to her. Francesca picked it up, unfolded it and started to read, and continued to read with growing dread. She reached the end of the news item; it was one she had missed. She checked the date, it had been published during her holiday, when she was out of Rome, at Sorrento, she and Dominic . . . she re-read the item, a taxi driver had been shot, murdered in his vehicle, in a street in central Rome, not too far from where she and Marco now sat. The incident had occurred in broad daylight. But it was the name of the murdered man which had startled her. She looked at Marco.

'That's right,' said Marco, grimly. 'It was Guiseppe. It must have been Pietro's doing. He was ruthless in the old days. His kind do not change. Others might be young, easily led, misguided, but the Pietros of this world never change.'

Francesca shook her head. 'It couldn't have been him,' she said flatly, 'why would he . . .?' She looked again at the paper as if by re-reading it she could change the details. 'Why would Pietro do something like this?'

'I don't know,' Marco spoke irritably, with all the irritation of a man under stress. 'Maybe Guiseppe was going to start talking, I never trusted him. He was weak. Anyway, we had better warn the others.'

'This wasn't Pietro's work,' Francesca tapped the newspaper. 'I just don't believe it. I refuse to believe it.'

'No, I didn't think that you would,' he replied wearily. 'Look, let's find somewhere more private. Come on and I'll get a taxi.'

Marco rose to his feet, scraping the chair noisily across the floor and left a handful of coins on the table as he departed. He walked towards the doorway and the hanging beads, the busy street and sweltering heat. Francesca remained at the table as if in a state of shock. Again, she re-read the newspaper item and slowly stood up, still reading the paper.

The man stood behind the circular newspaper stand. He held the briefcase in his left hand. He had sought a vantage point which also offered shade because the wig was uncomfortable to wear in the heat but, most importantly, he had to stay where he could observe the door of the café. The newspaper stand would do; it offered little, but sufficient shade, enough to keep him from fainting and it was less than fifteen metres from the doorway of the café. He knew that two of them were in there, one, the man he had followed, and the other the woman who, to his surprise and great delight, had joined him. The man pondered, and he thought that if they remained together then there would be no reason why he should not be able to nail them both. The 9mm in his briefcase would stop a charging horse, even with the silencer fitted. All it would require was one well placed round in the chest of each, that's all. Head shots were too dangerous in a situation like this, too many passers-by. He might hit a pedestrian and that would be an unwelcome complication. So it was going to be a chest shot, just like on the firing range, those cardboard cut-outs of soldiers with 'shoot here to kill' printed on their chests. A chest shot for each if he could manage it. He thought that he would be able to shoot one. Which one it didn't matter, women are just as easy to kill as men, he'd done it before, and the woman would be shot sooner or later, and so it might as well be now. He relished the thought of shooting both. If he could do that, then his already high credibility would be even higher.

Suddenly the man Marco appeared in the doorway, flinging the beads aside. He strode to the pavement and seemed to be looking for a taxi. The man in the wig opened his briefcase and, with a smooth, swift movement, took the 9mm and levelled it at Marco, sighting down the bulbous silencer until his target turned and presented his chest full on.

For a split second their eyes met.

For a split second a look of horror froze on Marco's face.

The weapon kicked, made a single, barely perceptible, 'phutt' sound and the man turned away, replacing the weapon in the briefcase less than five seconds after he had withdrawn it. He didn't bother to look behind him. He walked away, hearing first one female scream behind him then another, and another, then the beginnings of pandemonium.

Pity that he didn't get both, he thought, a great pity.

Two would have been neat and efficient, but it was all right, really all right. There was nowhere that the woman could go to hide, nowhere any of them could go; nowhere. And after ten years, another day or two wouldn't make any difference. It wouldn't make any difference at all.

*   *   *

She paced the floor of the room. The room which, to her taste, was drab and dull and functional. A room for cheap nights in more ways than one. The bed was hard and the wardrobe smelt of mothballs. She kept the light on. Earlier, as dusk had fallen, she had turned it off and had lain on the bed trying to calm herself, trying to come to terms with Marco's death, trying to get that fateful fleeting image out of her mind, the image of her old friend and comrade who had contacted her, to warn her. He had sat opposite her at the table in the café, planning a future, worried but still planning, planning in the first instance to take her somewhere safer, he said, no, private, that's it, somewhere more private. The next minute he was lying on the pavement, his shirt front not red, but black with blood and he was making awful, horrific gargling sounds. She had just been able to glimpse Marco for a moment before the surge of the crowd forced her away.

Gathering her wits and forcing herself to move, she

32

had left the place of death and taken a room in a cheap hotel. She had sat at the window, watched vacantly as the remainder of that day ebbed and, when dusk fell, she had left the window and lain on the bed. As darkness came so too came the penetrating and rapid tap, tap, tap of cockroaches crossing the floor. She turned the light on and sent the insects scurrying for the dark recesses where the walls of the room met the floor. Just a day, no, just six hours earlier the cockroaches would have upset her, bothered her. She would have complained, moved hotels, but now she was strangely unconcerned by their presence. So long as they remained in their holes and didn't come out into the room, that was all she was bothered about. She would just keep the light on until sleep became a necessity.

There was a knock on her door.

She turned rapidly, sat upright, startled. 'Who is it?' she demanded in a hushed whisper.

'Francesca,' returned a voice from outside the door, equally hushed, 'it's me, Guilo.'

She walked to the door silently in her stockinged feet and then stood to one side of the door frame. More than once in her life she had seen the ease with which bullets could penetrate a door; especially the doors of cheap hotels. 'What have you brought?' she asked, urgently.

'I've brought the books you wanted.'

She breathed deeply, sighing with relief, and opened the door just enough to let Guilo slide into the room.

They stood looking at each other. Ten years since they had last seen each other. She thought he hadn't changed, in those days he had been nineteen years old, with long hair and a long scarf, baggy loose fitting clothes; now he was twenty nine years old, and his appearance hadn't altered in the slightest. He was a perpetual student.

'Not the Hilton, is it?' he said when greetings and pleasantries had been exchanged.

'No, but at least I'm safe here.'

They stared at each other for a moment and then Guilo took a folded newspaper from his jacket pocket and handed it to her.

'Inside page,' he said. He let her begin to read and then told her, 'They say that the police don't have any leads.' He paused, allowing her to read the article in full, the article about Marco's death, about him being gunned down in the street.

'What do you think is going on?' he asked when she looked up from the newspaper.

'I don't know,' she replied, 'but I do know that that is two of us dead. You know how to reach Duccio still?'

'Yes.'

'Then warn him. Fast.'

Later, once again alone in the room, she sat on the bed and picked up the phone. She dialled and spoke and listened and waited and then she spoke again. She finished the conversation by saying, '. . . Mama will be home soon and that's a promise. Just be good and do what Grandmama says, . . . yes, and what Vincenzo says too. Goodnight. Goodnight.'

She hung up and rolled backwards onto the bed and stared up at the cracks in the ceiling. Pretty soon she would have to turn off the light, pretty soon the cockroaches would be able to have the floor all to themselves. She thought that they must have known they would anyway, it was just a question of nestling in and waiting. It was the same for her too, in a sense, just a question of waiting for a bullet in the head, any minute, any day, any week. Just a question of waiting.

Or was it? Was there not something that she could do. Was there not a place she could go to, away from Rome, away from Italy? Was there not a man in her life? A man to whom she could turn for help? A man who had the means to help her. If she could make him help her then she might survive.

She switched off the light. The cockroaches invaded the floor as if with pent-up impatience, filling the room with the clicking of their feet on the floor. She turned on one side and in the darkness began to draw up a plan.

Chapter 2

DOMINIC ROSSI STOOD in his driveway in the rain and surveyed his house, his recent acquisition. It had potential. He told himself that it had potential. In fact, he realised, that really was the only positive thing to be said about the building. It was a far cry from the Villa Arcalli on the outskirts of Rome.

His property was a large, imposing detached house, also, by coincidence, known in local parlance as a 'villa', though not at all on the same scale as the Villa Arcalli. It was, however, solid and located in the prosperous south side of the city of Glasgow. He stood in his gravel driveway, an overgrown garden, heavy with moisture, on either side of him and, after pausing to survey the house, crunched over the gravel towards the front door. As he approached the door, his eye was caught by the quality of the masonry between the door and the right hand downstairs window. He had not noticed it earlier; it looked rotten. He reached out and his fears were confirmed as the surface of the stone crumbled at his touch.

'It's got real potential,' he said as he turned the key in the lock. 'I mean real potential.' He told himself that he had to keep thinking that, he had to, otherwise the move from his loft in the Merchant City would begin to seem a dreadful mistake. House purchase can be like that, dreadful mistakes not easily rectified.

He unlocked the door and let himself into the building, his home, for all its shortcomings. The hallway was spartan, with buckets and plastic basins placed strategically to collect the rainwater where it dripped to the floor. The buckets, basins and tin pots were laid all along the hallway and extended up the stairs.

'Potential!' he said to himself. 'It's got real potential!' He left the hall and entered the living- room. It was the one room of the house he had rapidly made habitable and was at least comfortably furnished, mainly, if not wholly, with items of furniture from his old flat. He took off his coat, shook it and laid it down over the back of a chair and stood in the centre of the room, smart in a dark suit.

'It's me,' he shouted with a grin, amusing himself, listening to his voice echo in the empty, cavernous house.

'It's Dominic, the hunter home from the hill.' He put his briefcase down on the carpet. 'Oh, hello, Dominic. How was your day at the office? Tell me, Dominic, how did you get on in Edinburgh; of course you went to Edinburgh today, tell me all about it while I fix you a nice cup of tea, or would you prefer . . . .' his voice tailed off.

'Aye,' he said to himself, 'chance would be a fine thing.'

The front doorbell rang.

'No, no.' Rossi said, walking across the living room towards the door. 'I'll get it. Can we manage a few extra people for dinner?'

He left the drawing room and walked into the empty echoing hallway. He opened the front door, pulling it wide.

Gerry Cowan stood there in the rain, grinning. He had, as was usual, a bohemian appearance; long furry hair, flowing clothes, spectacles, scarf. He had not changed a great deal so far as Rossi could tell, in terms both of attitude and appearance, since they had been undergraduates together.

'Oh, it's yourself,' he said, grinning at Rossi, and, as Rossi stepped to one side, he entered the house. Cowan carried a six-pack of beer and two takeaway pizzas. 'Butler's night off, I suppose.'

'Funny you should mention servants opening doors,' said Rossi dryly, detecting his friend's bantering mood. 'I'll tell you a story sometime.'

'Tell me now, I'm always receptive to copy.'

'Sometime,' repeated Rossi. 'Six cans, well you really have pushed the boat out tonight, haven't you?'

'Well, I'm just a humble journalist of slender

means.' Cowan handed Rossi a copy of the *Glasgow Free Press*. Rossi accepted it and shut the door behind Cowan. 'I'm not a member of the propertied classes, if you can call this property.'

Cowan stood in the hallway and looked about him, especially at the basins and pots on the floor.

'Really, Dominic, I've seen ruined castles in better nick.' He paused again. 'Now, which is the nearest gentleman's rest room, the east wing or the west wing?'

'Can I take your coat, Gerry?'

Rossi slung Cowan's coat over the banister rail at the foot of the stair and led Cowan upstairs. 'I'm afraid that the west wing is closed to the public at the moment; the swimming-pool has been moved to the front of the house so that . . .'

'. . .the neighbours can get a better view.'

'Well, they do lead such drab lives.'

Cowan grinned, 'Well, the sight of you in the pool with your rubber duck will do wonders for their morale. The men's anyway.' He followed Rossi onto the landing where he noticed still more buckets, collecting still more rainwater. He handed the pizzas to Rossi and went into the bathroom. 'The guy who sold you this dump must be the estate agent of the year. No, I take that back, the decade.'

'It's a tactical investment.' Rossi remained at the door of the bathroom. 'By the time I sell it, I shall have enough profit to . . .'

'. . . to become one of Her Majesty's Advocates.' Cowan hovered over to the sunken bath. Rossi enjoyed the obvious difficulty with which Cowan concealed being impressed by the item.

'Took the wind out of your sails?' enquired Rossi, turning away, leaving Cowan to enjoy the gentleman's rest room.

Later, in a room completely empty except for a table tennis table, Cowan asked about Rossi's holiday.

'Lots of Club 18–30 rejects like yourself?' he said, provokingly.

'Thereby hangs a tale, but not one you'd believe. I'll tell you sometime, but it's hardly the adventures of a club what-not reject.'

'Those stories you're going to tell me sometime!'

'It's all one and the same story, in fact.'

'So tell, it's a rainy night outside, nowhere to go.'

'Sometime, I said, when you're in a different mood. Tell you one thing, though, it was two weeks blissfully free of politically biased journalists.'

'Well, I'm glad you raised that point, comrade. While you were off sunning yourself in Sorrento, a certain person's political career took a giant leap forward.'

Cowan pointed to the copy of the *Glasgow Free Press*. He opened two cans of beer, handed one to

Rossi and then proceeded to grapple with the packaging of the pizzas.

'In a fit of modesty, I stuck it on page two.'

Rossi read the report by Angus MacWheechie, one of Gerry's various pseudonyms. It recorded, reasonably objectively, that Gerry Cowan, the somewhat controversial journalist, had been selected as the prospective Parliamentary Labour candidate for Glasgow Woodside. The report further stated that Cowan was a surprise choice, given his suspected links with the Militant Tendency, but went on to imply rather neatly, Rossi thought, that Cowan represented the old honoured traditions of socialism and was, as such, greatly preferable to the Filofax Tendency.

'The guy's got a seven thousand majority, Gerry. And he's one of the best-known faces in the country.' Rossi accepted a slice of pizza. 'What chance have you got to knock him off his perch?'

'Plenty of time to get my act together.' Cowan ate his pizza, helping it down with beer. 'You see, there's probably two years to the next general election and given that a week is a long time in politics . . .,' he swallowed more beer, 'and so, Dominic, a little more respect for the newly elected Labour candidate for Glasgow Woodside.'

Rossi threw Cowan a blatantly disrespectful look and, putting down his can of beer, walked over to the table tennis table. He picked up a bat and began to bounce a ball on it.

'Win an election!' he said, keeping his eye on the ball. 'You can't even win at ping pong, let alone table tennis.'

Cowan rose to the challenge and Rossi lost.

Spectacularly.

'Concentration's the secret,' said Cowan, as they laid their bats down. 'Concentration. I told those Chinese guys that you were the sharpest lawyer in Glasgow.'

'What Chinese guys, for God's sake?' Rossi looked at Cowan.

'Just some clients I'm sending your way.' Cowan walked from the table, leant down, grabbed a can of beer and tore it open. 'A very important section of my future constituents, the Chinese community. So, don't screw it up.'

'So what's their problem?' Rossi sat on the floor against the wall next to Cowan and joined him in a beer. 'The boys on the night beat demanding free takeaways every night?'

'Something to do with buying new premises. I told them you were . . .' Cowan glanced around him, '. . . a property expert.'

*   *   *

Later, when Cowan had left, Rossi lay in bed, his

hands clasped behind his head. Sleep eluded him. His mind drifted to Italy, it drifted to the beach, to that brief moment when he had first seen her and, even then, it had only been by sheer good fortune that he did so. Looking up from his prone position out of curiosity, levering himself up onto his elbows and turning his head to find out why all the men around him, all the 'beach bums' were nudging each other in barely constrained excitement. Then he too had stared at her, a sophisticated woman in her prime, a woman of breathtaking beauty who was stepping gracefully and nimbly across the sand, beach towel in one hand and suntan lotion in the other, and who was wearing the smallest pale green bikini. His mind had drifted to the incident later that day, in the early evening when he had seen her in the foyer of the hotel and he recalled the thump in his chest when he had realised that she too was a fellow guest. His mind drifted to the bar of the hotel, that evening, after dinner; when he had seen her sitting alone, elegant in red, and approached her.

His mind drifted to the delectable Francesca Arcalli.

*   *   *

The courts within the newly built Sheriff Court's complex at Carlton Place, Glasgow, never failed to remind Rossi of a cinema. Gone were the old hard benches, replaced in the new building by rows of upholstered seats in a delicate shade of grey. Gone was the Sheriff's high bench, replaced by a lower, but no less dignified, version in pine. Gone too were the severe columned walls and highly vaulted ceilings of the old court in Brunswick Street. The new court had walls of a light pastel shade and the ceilings were lower. It was in fact a false ceiling, the lights which illuminated the court shone softly through opaque perspex panels. The false ceiling was made of light-weight materials, designed to 'give' in the event of a bomb blast, thus allowing the explosion to dissipate rather than be contained. The late twentieth century was a troubled time and terrorism was a threat to be taken seriously.

Rossi entered the court, bowed to the bench, and sat discreetly at the rear of the room listening intently to the proceedings, to the court room drama, as it unfolded before him. The Sheriff was an elderly man. He sat in a black gown, one hand cupping his head while he took notes with the other. The man in the dock stood with his feet apart, hands clasped together behind his back, not speaking, not moving, but listening intently, not at all relaxed. Wilful fire-raising is a serious crime. By contrast, the man giving evidence seemed to Rossi to be very relaxed, very self-assured. Too self-assured by far for Rossi's liking. It didn't sit well with the man's hard, mean face. Rossi thought that if this particular witness wasn't a cop, he'd be a villain.

He sat in the Sheriff Court, listening to the closing questions of the Depute Procurator Fiscal, a small but stocky young man, who Rossi had found to be unashamedly careerist.

'Thank you, Detective Inspector,' said the careerist Depute Procurator Fiscal. 'No further questions.'

Rossi had arrived at his office that morning, to be met by the bustling Shona, enquiring about his day in Edinburgh and placing the post and a cup of coffee on his desk. He had evaded the question about Edinburgh, countering with a question about the events in the office during his absence. 'Hectic,' had been Shona's snappy reply.

He had sought out Eleanor Goodchild, his junior partner. Severely dressed in a grey suit, she was dictating to her clerk in the reception area.

'Eleanor, I need to talk to you,' he had said, interrupting her, a certain rudeness on his part he hoped being excused by necessity and urgency. But she had swept out of the office saying she was due in court.

Rossi had turned to the clerk. 'What case?'

'The wilful fire-raising, sir,' Paul had replied nervously, 'otherwise known as Ally the arsonist.'

Rossi had returned to his desk, drunk his coffee, glanced at the mail. Eleanor Goodchild had come to the practice with impeccable credentials, she was

45

efficient in matters of administration, in legal discussion she had shown that she knew her stuff, she had a personality which was strong but not abrasive or over-powering; ideal for working in a small office. But Rossi had never seen her plead in the Sheriff Court. So, he had left his offices, walked onto Clyde Street, marvelling at what he felt to be a superb frontage of buildings on the south bank of the river, extending from the new Sheriff Court to Pollokshaws Road. He had crossed the river by the suspension footbridge, entered the Sheriff Court building, wide, light and airy, and found his way to Court Two itself, taking his seat just as the Depute Procurator Fiscal said '. . . no further questions.'

Rossi shifted slightly in his seat as the Sheriff raised his eyes towards Eleanor Goodchild.

'Miss Goodchild,' he said, in a soft voice of authority.

'Thank you, my Lord.' Eleanor Goodchild stood and paused before addressing the man who stood confidently in the witness stand. When she spoke, she spoke in measured, balanced tones. 'In your long experience, Inspector Ballantyne, have you dealt frequently with crimes involving wilful fire-raising?'

'Over the years,' Ballantyne rocked slightly in his heels, 'yes, I have.'

The slight movement made by the Detective Inspector gave Rossi the impression of a large and powerfully built man. Even for a policeman.

'It would therefore be fair to assume,' continued Goodchild, 'would it not, that you know a considerable amount about the techniques involved?'

Rossi became intrigued. He already saw a trap beginning to open for Ballantyne. She was good all right. She'd do.

'Well,' said Ballantyne, allowing himself a small smirk, 'I wouldn't call myself an expert.'

'Oh, come on, Detective Inspector,' Goodchild smiled, becomingly, calculatingly, fatally, 'don't be so modest.'

'Miss Goodchild,' the Sheriff leaned forward and spoke with an element of irritation. 'I believe the Crown has already been at some pains to establish the witness's credentials as an experienced police officer.'

The Depute Fiscal made the most of this point. He rose and said, smugly, 'My Lord, I don't object to the defence's attempts to treat Detective Inspector Ballantyne as an expert.'

Rossi's pulse raced, a bead of sweat trickled from his scalp, she now had three of them dancing on the end of a string; if she lost her composure now she would lose everything.

The Sheriff nodded to Goodchild to continue. Goodchild cleared her throat, speaking in her own good time.

'So,' she said, 'when you went to my client's house

acting on . . .' she paused for good dramatic effect, knowing that a good trial lawyer is first and foremost a good actor. (Rossi knew she knew that because he had told her so.) '. . . information received,' and delivered the last two words with a dry derisiveness, glancing at the defendant as she did so, 'you knew exactly what you were looking for.'

Ballantyne's eyes widened; he saw the trap that Rossi had seen a few minutes earlier. 'Well, in a general way, yes,' he said, nervously.

Rossi, sitting at the rear of the court, smiled discreetly; the performance that Goodchild was turning in took backbone and emotional stamina. She also knew how to demolish credibility. You don't chip away from top to bottom with a hammer and chisel, you remove a brick from the foundations and stand clear. Easy when you know how and this girl was a natural.

'In a general way, I see.' Goodchild paused. 'Mr Ballantyne, do you recall a case of fire raising which you investigated in March of last year? In Springfield Road?'

'I don't have the notes in front of me,' Ballantyne stammered evasively. Rossi thought of him like a cornered prey, perhaps not quite cornered, not yet, but it was only a matter of time and Rossi detected the cheetah in the grey suit gathering speed as she homed in for the kill.

'Fortunately,' she said, 'I have here a copy of the inventory of productions in that case.' Goodchild addressed the Sheriff. 'My Lord, I conducted the prosecution in that case to which I am referring.'

Goodchild took papers from the desk in front of her and handed copies to the Clerk of the Court who handed them to the Sheriff. The Clerk handed a third copy to Ballantyne who accepted them grudgingly. The Depute Fiscal slouched in his chair, angered.

Goodchild allowed the Sheriff and Ballantyne time to read and digest the information contained in the notes. Then she spoke, not at all hurriedly.

'The items,' she said, 'retrieved from the house of the accused in that case are identical with the items produced in this case, are they not, Inspector Ballantyne? Not in a general way, but identical?'

'It appears so,' conceded Ballantyne, weakly.

'So,' Goodchild picked up speed, 'what you allegedly found in my client's house was exactly what you were looking for?'

'I don't accept the implication of the question,' Ballantyne snapped aggressively, cornered, desperate. Goodchild paused and Rossi winced in sheer delight as the trap closed.

'What implication?' asked Goodchild, sweetly. Ballantyne flushed with anger and self-irritation. He shot a glance at the Depute Fiscal, a get-me-out-of-this-mess plea.

The Fiscal rose to speak, but the Sheriff said, 'The witness will answer the question.' It was said so mildly but the implications echoed in the hushed court room.

It was, Rossi thought, a good illustration of the maxim that the less you speak, the more you say and the softer you speak, the more you are heard. 'Witness will answer the question,' were words said softly, with economy of speech, yet they were words which nailed Ballantyne.

'The implication that,' Ballantyne swallowed,' . . . the implication that . . . the evidence was . . .'

'Planted?' Goodchild helped him. 'Was that the word you were searching for? Let's move on, Detective Inspector. Have you ever arrested my client before?'

'Er . . .' Ballantyne was startled. This was something else he had not anticipated.

'Oh, come, Mr Ballantyne,' Goodchild pressed him sharply, 'I'm quite prepared to concede that my client has felt the long arm of the law before.' She pressed her question. 'Have you ever arrested my client before?'

'Yes,' said Ballantyne, crossly.

'How often?'

'Five times.'

'How many convictions were secured?'

'One,' said Ballantyne, flatly.

Goodchild paused, then said, 'And am I right in believing that you secured this conviction the first time that you arrested him?'

'That's correct,' Ballantyne replied, flushed with anger, restraining himself and, thought Rossi, clearly feeling an acute sense of humiliation.

'My client,' said Goodchild, relishing her victory, 'could therefore be said, could he not, to be your favourite suspect . . .?'

Rossi edged his way to the aisle, bowed to the bench, turned and left the court. He had heard enough and grinned with satisfaction. 'And there, members of the jury,' he said to himself as he pushed the door open, 'goes the ball game.'

*   *   *

The man with the wolf's face expression walked away from the scene, regaining his composure. It's the way of it sometimes, he told himself, nothing he could blame himself for. The boys who had snatched his briefcase were a long way off now, at the far side of the park. All he wanted to do now was to get the wretched wig off his head. It itched insufferably in the heat. He followed the path out of the park, leaving by the entrance he had entered just a few minutes earlier. He was leaving the park, in order to fight another day, but when he had entered he had been following, nay stalking, his prey among the wide paths, the grass and the tall cypress trees.

He had stalked them, two of them, from the moment that they met outside the post office. He had followed the man that he knew only as Guilo, followed him for most of the day and, when he saw him apparently waiting outside the post office at the top of the square, Carlo too decided to wait. It was a gamble. It was a gamble that the man Guilo wouldn't see him, wouldn't become suspicious, wouldn't be able to give a description. It was part of that gamble that he missed the opportunity to dispose of Guilo, for there he had been, a sitting target, standing against a wall, nobody around, the town beginning its siesta. He could have done it, even made it a head shot. But he was curious, a policeman's instinct, curious about why Guilo was waiting, about who or what was he waiting for.

It had been ten years since the bomb, ten years since the family had died, blown up as they drove down the road. Ten years is a long time, but again, as in the case of the woman, one or two days would not make a great deal of difference. And besides, they were jumpy, their past was catching up with them, casting long shadows. It would do them no harm to sweat.

'Take your time, Carlo,' Cristaldi had said to him at the beginning. 'You are good at your job and remember, as our ancestors have said for centuries, "revenge is a dish best taken cold", so be Italian about this, Carlo, savour the dish cold and eat slowly and thoroughly, but eat.'

So, he had waited and then the man he recognised from the files, and who he knew only as Duccio, joined Guilo. One conspirator had become two.

He had moved his briefcase from his right hand to his left. They started to walk, a car passed between him and the conspirators. He followed.

They walked out of the square.

They walked down a cobbled street where a woman in black sat in her front doorway, saying nothing, seeing all.

They talked as they walked. Carlo could not hear them. He kept a safe distance, but he could tell by their gestures that they were agitated. They were demonstrative, even for Italians; they gesticulated wildly and shot questioning glances at each other, but not behind them, fortunately for Carlo, not behind them. If either of those two men, both in their thirties, both untidily dressed, had glanced behind them, and seen the tall, coldly predatory man with a fine head of hair and a briefcase in his hand . . .

But they had not turned.

They entered the park.

Perfect, could not be better.

Carlo had increased his pace.

A park, isolated during the siesta, he had thought it could not have been easier than if he had hailed the two men, given them the gun and invited them to shoot themselves.

Then the boys had appeared. Three of them. He would wait until they had passed, they were a nuisance but not an obstacle. They were children. About twelve years old, he guessed.

But they were good. Very good. Gave him no signals whatsoever, no tell-tale looks, didn't look at him at all. Maybe that in itself ought to have told him something. As they drew level with him, one, the nearest, had grabbed the briefcase with both hands and tugged it from his grip.

They ran. He pursued. But they were twelve years old. He was in early middle age. The gap increased and when they were perhaps a hundred metres from him, the boy who had snatched the briefcase opened it as he ran. Carlo knew what the boy had seen: a 9mm automatic with silencer.

The boy stopped, as if arrested by an invisible rope. His friends ran on. The boy dropped the briefcase and its sinister contents and ran after his friends.

Carlo picked up the case, checked the contents, closed it and walked out of the park. To an onlooker it would have appeared a simple, distasteful bag snatch. But the boy had seen the gun, children chatter, even if they are not believed.

Time to go, he had told himself, the dish remains cold and there's plenty of time yet to savour it.

Chapter 3

ROSSI LEFT the Sheriff Court building, turned left and walked back across the suspension bridge. He enjoyed the cityscape before him, the spectacular Catholic Cathedral, the buildings which nestled sensitively against one another, the pub on the waterfront, the black and white hull of the Carrick, perhaps Glasgow's premier restaurant, at her berth, to his right. He enjoyed the stroll back to his place of work, impressed with Eleanor Goodchild's performance, confident that she would be a great asset to the team, although he thought that she needed a wider work experience. Keenness is all very well, but experience is what carries the day. He entered his office and nodded to Shona who was on the phone but raised her hand in greeting as he entered.

He walked into his office and picked up the pile of papers, the afternoon mail delivery, the telephone messages which had accumulated in his in-tray during his absence. He sat at his desk and scanned the papers, digesting the information offered by some, scribbling a note to be typed in response to others and placing the rest in a 'pending' file. He stood and walked to a filing cabinet which stood at the far corner of his room, sifted through the files in the drawer and, finding the one he was looking for, removed it from the drawer and returned to his seat, laying the file on the desk top in front of him. He untied the red ribbon which bound the file, opened it and began to read. An hour later, he was still engrossed in the file, a complex conveyancing, when the door of his office was flung open. Eleanor Goodchild stood in the doorway, grinning, leaning against the handle.

'Next case!' she said, holding her free hand upraised with thumb and forefinger together in a gesture of triumph.

'Another professional wilful fire-raiser, ready for the next bankrupt, I take it?' Rossi leaned back in his chair. His tone was deliberately muted. She was good, she was damned good, he'd already decided that, but he didn't want to go overboard with praise.

'So,' Goodchild said after a pause caused by the unexpectedly clipped tones of the senior partner. 'How did you like the way I got that flash cop on the ropes?'

'It was neat.' Rossi conceded. 'Very neat, indeed.'

Goodchild stood up straight in the doorway and assumed a haughty attitude. 'Have you been smoking again?' she asked, disapprovingly, changing the subject suddenly.

'It must have been a client.' He dismissed the

observation. 'Close the door, will you, please.' Eleanor Goodchild stepped into the office. She closed the door behind her and leaned against it. She looked at Rossi questioningly.

'I've got something to tell you,' he said. 'I'd like a word about a couple of things.'

'Like you're thinking of becoming an advocate.'

Rossi shot a startled glance towards her and then leaned back in his chair.

'It was inevitable,' she said, by means of explanation. 'I mean that running a firm's not your style, is it? You haven't been comfortable as a senior partner, you've made that plain. You see, Dominic, people like you, well they need to be subordinate because it's only in a junior or subordinate position that they can develop their basic cavalier attitude to the full. You can't be a rebel if you're in charge of the ship.'

She cocked her head to one side and smiled. 'Seniority, authority, well they have too many expectations, too much restriction for a maverick like you, Dominic. You need something to kick against.' She saw by Dominic Rossi's thoughtful look that she was reaching him. She pressed her point home.

'We used to play a game at university, trying to identify someone we knew, if this person was an animal what sort of animal would he be, if this person was a landscape, what sort of landscape would she be, and so on. If someone who was happy being a senior partner was an animal, then that person would be a lion, with a pride of lionesses about him who did all the work, while he sunned himself and fought off the occasional predatory male, but that's not you Dominic. If you were an animal, you'd be a rogue male elephant, quite happy to forage alone, doing what you think is right and not necessarily needing the rest of the herd for protection or decision making. Looks like I'd better start looking for a new partner, because finding her is not going to be easy.'

'Her?' said Rossi, still reeling from Goodchild's barrage of home truths, still devastated by her perception. She'd been going round with her eyes open all right.

'A new partner for me,' she continued, smiling. 'Poor Dominic, do you have visions of a monstrous regiment of women.'

'*Regimen,*' Rossi corrected her and did so with no small amount of irritation. 'It's a Latin word.'

'Thank you,' Eleanor Goodchild said primly, 'my classical education was not wholly neglected.'

'Still, it's incorrect to say regiment. It has nothing to do with armies. Knox was referring to the rule of women.'

'It's amazing to see what frustration does. You're becoming a pedant, Dominic. You know, the sooner that you get your advocate's bits and bobs and get back into crime, the better.'

'You're probably right. So tell me, madam junior partner, how did you hear about my career change? From my mentor, Sinclair Murray, perhaps?'

Eleanor turned and opened the door of Rossi's office. She turned back and grinned at him, over her shoulder. 'Gavin McKenzie saw you coming out of the Clerk's office in the Advocates' Library in Edinburgh last week and put two and two together. It's a small world, the world of the law, especially in Scotland.' She left his office, closing the door behind her.

Rossi leaned forward, closed the file in front of him and re-tied the ribbon. He calculated twenty seconds, thirty at the outside. In fact, she was back in fifteen, flinging his door wide.

'And who, may I ask,' she entered his office with a flourish, 'are the two Chinese gentlemen out there waiting to see me?'

'Oh, them,' said Rossi, smiling, 'They're just opening a new restaurant and they're looking for premises.' He paused and then continued, blandly, 'I thought that you'd enjoy a bit of conveyancing work.'

'Conveyancing! Me! After the performance I turned in this morning, it's obvious that I'm a good criminal lawyer.'

'A solicitor has to be versatile, especially a junior partner. You need to widen your experience.' He continued in a more serious tone. 'Anyway, don't knock it. If we can get ourselves known within the

Chinese community, it's worth a hell of a lot of business, and the rent has to be paid, one way or another.'

He paused, 'And as the junior partner, it is the kind of thing that you are really supposed to be doing, instead of making a name for yourself on the criminal side. So, if you'd see the Chinese gentlemen, please, and . . .' he picked up the file which he had been reading, 'I'd also like you to address yourself to this. As you'll see, it's a conveyancing which has been going on for some time. It's a new property. Our client wants to buy, the owner, the builder, wants to sell.'

'So, what's the problem? The price?'

'No, the price is agreed. The trouble is, it turns out that he built it in perhaps not the most appropriate place.'

'Meaning?'

'Meaning that there's a public right of way which more or less runs through the living room.'

'Oh.'

'Yes, there's a few ramblers' associations up in arms about it, especially as the right of way is as ancient as the hills. The adjacent landowners won't hear of it being re-routed over their property. It'll require delicate negotiations with the Scottish Office. The bottom line is that the building will have to be demolished, so do what you can, please . . . that is, once you've attended to Mr Wang and Mr Chen.'

She closed his door with a slam.

*   *   *

Rossi left his office at 6.00 p.m. and drove home to his rambling house. Seeing it in the fading light, he told himself once again that it had potential.

'Real potential,' he said, unlocking the front door and letting himself into the hallway. He bent down and picked up his mail from behind the front door, just two bills and both red. He walked to the rear of the house to the kitchen, a modern kitchen which he had had fitted shortly after moving into the house. He had favoured dark stained wood and a black plastic working surface. A pine table with matching pine farmhouse chairs stood in the centre of the room. A telephone hung on the wall, close to the door.

He dropped the bills onto the table and looked out of the kitchen window into the small back garden. A children's swing left by the previous owner stood to the left and beyond the wall was a spectacular view across the City of Glasgow. Just two red bills waiting for him; he'd hoped for more, it had been well over a week now, he ought to have heard from her by now. But, in fairness, he hadn't written to her, not having had time has always been a lame excuse for not coming up with the goods, he thought, so no, he wouldn't be hypocritical. He'd pen a loving letter this weekend, plenty of time, the weekend, just re-jig the list of 'things to do' and put 'letter to Francesca' at the top. He opened the cupboards and looked at the choice of tinned food. He began to compose the letter to Francesca in his head.

He ate hurriedly. A poor quality meal has to be bolted down if it is to be eaten at all. He ate without satisfaction and then sat in his living-room, digesting the meal and re-arranging the order of jobs to be done, with the letter to Francesca being the most urgent.

Around mid-evening, he left his house and took a taxi into the city. He went to the Advocates' Bar and entered the highly polished, carpeted interior with its smartly turned out waiters. The only noise was the low hum of learned conversation. He paused, looked around the room and, in the far corner, saw Sinclair Murray sitting, apparently enjoying a conversation with another man Rossi did not recognise. He made his way over to them, weaving between tables, stood at a respectful distance from their table and asked:

'Am I interrupting?'

'No, no, not at all,' Sinclair Murray put the papers they were discussing down on the highly polished surface of the table and smiled at Rossi. 'It's just a strategy session. Sorry, do you know each other?'

Rossi shook his head and the second man stood, extending his right hand. Rossi saw he was in his early thirties, attractive looking and very fit courtesy of the legal profession. The man was tall and had chiselled, angular features.

'Rory Stuart-Frazer,' said Sinclair Murray. 'Dominic Rossi. Rory and I are sharing a murder trial next month. I've got the husband, he's got the mistress. It's the story of my life.'

'Do I hear a rumour that you are thinking of joining us chaps in Edinburgh?' Stuart-Frazer shook Rossi's hand warmly. Rossi thought the man affable, very upper middle class, very 'green wellie brigade', very Range Rover and possibly a small estate of about 1200 acres or so, somewhere near Perth.

'Been thinking about it,' replied Rossi as he sat down.

'One thing you should know if you are,' Stuart-Frazer smiled and leaned down, to Rossi's surprise and tapped Rossi's feet. 'Never wear brown shoes south of Perth if you are going to join us, Mr Rossi. Well, I have to leave you gentlemen. I don't want to get too late a train back to Edinburgh.' He stood. 'Goodnight, Alistair, Mr Rossi.'

Rossi watched Stuart-Frazer walk casually and leisurely out of the bar, stopping now and again to speak to people he recognised as he passed by their table. Rossi shook his head wearily.

Sinclair Murray signalled to the waiter. 'Never mind,' he said, 'it's called complacency, all lawyers suffer from it once they get to a certain stage in their career and it doesn't take long to get to the five figure fee stage. I'll buy you a small libation and we shall drink a toast to Sorrento and to memories of your Italian adventure. I'd like to hear about it. You seem to have changed since you came back.'

The waiter approached their table. Rossi leaned forward and toyed with the coasters while Sinclair Murray gave the order. The waiter left and Sinclair Murray turned to Rossi and studied his troubled expression.

'She must have made quite an impact,' he said at length.

'Yeah,' said Rossi, 'she did, but holiday romances don't last.' He paused. 'It's not that, at least, not just that. It's all such a mess at the moment, Alistair. I don't like the work I'm doing; my junior partner . . .'

'The dynamic Ms Goodchild?'

'The one and the same; well she's good, I respect her, but there's friction in our working relationship. If she was a man, I'd say that she was 'cocky'. I don't know what the female equivalent would be, but you know what I mean. I've just bought a new house, well it's not new, it's a wreck. A friend said that he'd seen ruined castles in better nick, and I keep telling myself that it's got potential . . . I had a fabulous flat with a roof-top patio in the Merchant City so I sold it for a run-down, crumbling, gothic monstrosity with a leaking roof. Now, why would I want to do that. Alistair, why on earth would I want to do a thing like that? But perhaps it's just that I'm insane. I mean if that's the case, then I'm happy, but it's the thought that I'm in full possession of my faculties and still did what I did that worries me. And the solution to all these problems is joining the Rory Stuart-Frazers "if you scratch my back, you can bring down grouse with my Purdeys" of this world. How the hell did a regular Glasgow guy like me get into this position, Alistair?'

'I believe it's called life,' replied Sinclair Murray as the waiter brought the drinks. He placed Rossi's on the coaster in front of him. Rossi reached for it and sank it in one.

'So they say,' said Rossi. 'Fancy making a night of it?'

' 'fraid not.' Sinclair Murray gathered his papers. 'It doesn't do for an advocate to get caught out too late; don't want to be on the streets when the pubs close.' He slid his papers into his briefcase. 'Listen, Dominic, take a tip from an older man, will you. Your problems don't sound like problems to me, so less carping. So you don't like your job, well join ninety per cent of the working population, and I emphasise the working population. Your junior partner's good, so you have a difficult relationship, you find her pushy. Would you rather have a dimwitted piece of deadwood? And you've bought one of the biggest houses in Glasgow which needs a little bit of work like every other

Victorian house in the UK. So what's your problem? You know what's really wrong with you, Dominic?' Sinclair Murray stood.

'No, what?'

'You're in love. I know, I've been there myself. Go ahead and make a night of it, it'll probably be one of your last opportunities to do so.'

'What do you mean?' Rossi looked up at the well dressed Sinclair Murray.

'Because, dear boy, I hear the sound of wedding bells, even if you don't. But wedding bells are a bit like bullets. You never hear the one that gets you. So they say. Goodnight. Oh, by the way, he was right about the shoes.'

Sinclair Murray left the bar, sweeping out with an authoritative walk. Rossi remained seated and toyed with his empty glass. He'd got the taste. He wanted a drink, he wanted to sink a good bucket tonight. He went up to the bar and levered himself onto a vacant stool. Hey, why not? He was drinking alone, so he'd drink alone, wad of notes and piles of coins in front of him, elbows on the bar, cigarette and a glass; just like a proper barstool turkey.

*   *   *

Rossi made it to work the next day.

Just.

His body felt as though it was half its normal size,

66

his head felt as though it was splitting open in two neat halves and his throat felt like the bottom of a budgie's cage, but he made it to work. Just. A bit late, but he got in.

By mid-morning and after not a few black coffees, his mind was beginning to focus. He was even able to retain what he read, chomping extra strong mints as he did so. At eleven a.m., he felt *compos mentis* enough to dictate. He summoned a very disapproving Shona who sat, huffily, at a greater distance than normal. She had also left the door of his office ajar, a further pointed sign of her disapproval of the alcoholic excesses indulged in by the senior partner.

Rossi dictated slowly, more slowly than necessary, finding it difficult to focus his thoughts to cope with the increasing tension between him and Shona. He was saved by Eleanor Goodchild; and by Benny MacLawrie.

He looked out onto the reception area and saw Eleanor Goodchild sweep across the floor, neatly dressed in a pinstripe suit and holding a black brief-case. She glanced into Rossi's office and hailed him.

'Off to inspect Chinese restaurants,' she called, 'back after lunch, which I trust will be on the house. Bye.' She stepped towards the door, rising to the challenge of conveyancing despite her protestations of yesterday. Rossi wondered if there was any stopping the girl.

'Bon appétit,' he said.

'How do you spell that?' asked Shona, sniffily.

'No,' Rossi faltered. 'I was speaking to . . .' he looked up and out into the reception area. It was as if timed to perfection; Eleanor opened the door, just as Benny MacLawrie was about to push it open from the outside, while trying to light a cigarette with a stubborn lighter. Benny stepped into the room as if the door had been opened for him, still trying to get a flame from the lighter. Rossi heard the exchange.

'Sorry, hen,' said MacLawrie, not looking at Goodchild, being utterly preoccupied with his lighter.

'I'm a person, Benny,' Goodchild flushed with anger. 'Not a farmyard fowl.' Then she stamped her foot. Angrily.

'Oh, hiya, Ms Goodchild.' Benny turned. He was a small, wiry man, with a flat cap, in his forties. He always seemed to wear a jacket and Rossi could not picture him in a raincoat, even in the rain. He sat back as he enjoyed the exchange and wondered, curiously, what it was that had brought Benny MacLawrie, a general rogue, reformed housebreaker, but who still retained his window-turning skill, to his door. Rossi thought of MacLawrie as a spark with no flame, a bit like his cigarette lighter in fact. MacLawrie continued to speak to Goodchild, no doubt, thought Rossi, with a whisky laden breath.

'I didnae see you there. How's it going working for Mr Rossi?'

Rossi winced and put his hand to his forehead.

'I am not working for Mr Rossi,' Goodchild said coldly and menacingly, staring straight into the eyes of the hapless Benny MacLawrie. She continued to growl, 'We are partners, Benny, you know partners, that means we work together. When you learn to read, look it up in a dictionary.'

'Aye,' Benny gave up with his lighter, but not with the angered Eleanor Goodchild. 'But he's been at it longer than you.' He smiled half-apologetically, but only half.

'When it comes to being "at it", as is the old Glasgow expression,' she said with controlled fury, but, thought Rossi, realising that she was flogging a dead horse, 'neither of us can hold a candle to you.' Goodchild turned tightly on her heels and marched out of the office.

'Not bad, Benny,' thought Rossi, as he watched MacLawrie walk across the reception area towards Paul's desk momentarily disappearing from his sight. 'At least you held your own, which is probably more than I could have done.'

'Now,' he said, 'where were we?'

'Letter to Alexander and Co., Mr Rossi,' said Shona, shortly. 'Property at Hamilton Park Avenue.'

'Oh, yes . . . In the event of any . . . this is Item 11

. . . in the event of any alterations having been carried out . . . carried out.' Rossi picked up his flow, '. . . to the Subjects, requiring planning permission, building warrant and/or Superior's consent, it is of the essence of the contract to follow hereon that all relevant certificates of planning permission, building warrants . . .'

There was a tap on his door. Rossi glanced up. 'Yes, Paul,' he said.

'There's a Mr MacLawrie here, Mr Rossi,' said Paul, awkwardly, and looking gauche in his first suit. 'He doesn't have an appointment,' continued Paul, nervously, apologetically, 'but . . .'

Benny MacLawrie slid between Paul and the door frame and entered Rossi's office. He stood grinning at Rossi and at the utterly exasperated Shona. Paul glanced at MacLawrie with ill-disguised irritation. MacLawrie turned and winked at Paul.

'. . . but he said that you'll see him anyway.'

'Oh, for God's sake, Benny.' Rossi sat back in his chair and nodded a 'we'll finish this later' nod to Shona, who collected her pad and notes and left the office, following Paul back into the reception area. She shut the door behind her just sufficiently hard enough to not be accused of slamming it. 'So,' said Rossi, 'what have you been up to now?'

'Not me, Mr Rossi,' Benny MacLawrie sounded upset that he could be thought of as a ne'er do well.

'It's my wee nephew. My sister's boy.'

'I hope he's loaded,' said Rossi. 'I come expensive these days. So take a seat and tell me about it.'

Benny MacLawrie sat as invited and, as he did so, he instantly cast an appreciative eye on a paperweight which lay on Rossi's desk. Rossi, equally instantly, took the weight and placed it safely in his desk drawer.

'Expensive?' Benny MacLawrie raised an eyebrow. 'I thought that we traded, you and I. We don't have a lot of money as a family, and so thought that I could ask you a sort of favour, Mr Rossi? Even the score. Know what I mean?'

'No, Benny,' said Rossi, slowly, seriously. 'I don't know what you mean. Tell me.'

'Well,' MacLawrie shifted uncomfortably in his seat. He sensed that his gambit hadn't been perhaps the most sensible or the most tactful. 'You remember that Pole, what was his name? Sadowski, or something, was that it? You remember you and me going into his house, a wee bit of opening lock-fast premises? Remember?'

'Benny,' Rossi leaned forward and looked intently at MacLawrie. 'That was what we call in the trade "a private moment". It's in your interest, in your extreme good interest, not to hold it over me.

'What do you mean, Mr Rossi?'

'What I mean, Benny, is that it works like this. I

don't forget favours, and I haven't forgotten that one. I don't forget people who do me favours, and I haven't forgotten you. But, and it's a big "but", I don't cave in to threats.'

'I didn't mean . . .'

'I don't care what you meant, Benny. You wouldn't be threatening or coercing me, Benny? Otherwise you and I will discontinue "to trade", as you call it.'

'Very good, Mr Rossi. I really didn't mean . . .'

'All right Benny, but just remember that. And since madam is out, I'll have a cigarette if I may?'

'Sure,' MacLawrie fumbled with his packet of Players. 'I'm afraid my lighter . . .'

Rossi produced a box of matches from the drawer and tossed them to Benny who caught the box, extracted a match, lit it and held the flame to his cigarette, all with a deft flick of the wrist.

'Tell me about it. What's this about your sister's wee boy?'

*   *   *

The man Carlo walked slowly. He was aware of the two *carabinieri* sitting in the Alfa Romeo, watching him from where they had parked. He was unconcerned by them. He knew that they were doing nothing more than their job. He was a pedestrian and they watched him pass for no other reason than that there was no other pedestrian to watch. Had he not been wearing the wig, then they might have recognised him. Had they known about the silenced automatic skilfully concealed beneath his light summer jacket, then they would have stopped him. Or at least tried to stop him.

Carlo, Carlo the assassin, with the hungry, wolf-like expression, walked slowly, methodically, purposefully. He walked with his mind focused on one job, doing it in his mind, before actually doing it with his body. It was the way he walked when he was going to kill somebody, slowly, as his mind programmed his body in preparation for the act, so that when the time came, he could act with detached precision. It was this honing of the mind and the body which had made him a cold, coolly efficient killer.

He walked beneath the dingy apartment block which stood in the part of the city where newspapers blow in the streets, where people sleep on the pavements, where dogs move in packs, where the refuse goes uncollected. To one side of him was the wall of the apartment block, the windows of the ground floor apartments breaking up the dull plasterwork. Occasionally, there was a face at the window, but only occasionally. To the other side of him was the street, with the parked cars nosed into the kerb at an angle. Between him and the kerb was a row of small trees, growing out of dusty plots between paving slabs. Behind him, now, at the top of the street, sat the two *carabinieri* in the Alfa Romeo.

Carlo mused briefly, in a lapse of concentration, how fortunate that the *carabinieri* had not stopped him to search him. If they had, he would have shot them; pawns in the fortunes of war.

He turned into the street door of the apartment building. The doorkeeper was absent. It wouldn't have mattered if she had seen him, but the fact that she wasn't there was an additional bonus. He walked up the stairs, padding silently on rubber soles. He moved stealthily, silently, like a cat.

There was no one about. The staircase was empty. The long corridors leading off the stairs to left and right were empty. It was always like that at mid-morning, which was why Carlo had chosen this hour to attack; the people who lived in this apartment building and in apartment buildings like it, were at their work now, at their domestic duties or at their studies. A few would be sitting alone in their rooms; the elderly, the infirm, the frightened politicos whose past was reaching up and patting them on their shoulder from behind . . . He left the stairs at the second floor and walked along the corridor, the front doors of the apartments on either side of him.

At one door, at one particular pre-identified door, he halted. He glanced around. No one in sight. He put his hand inside his jacket and reached for the automatic. He eased the safety-catch off and then tapped softly, almost childlike on the door. It was the oldest trick in the book, about as old as putting your hat on the end of a stick and poking it in the air to draw fire. And it always worked. The trick lay in not overdoing it.

Inside the apartment, Duccio sat in the chair by the bed. Above him and to one side were the Marxist posters he always took with him from flat to flat, from squat to squat. Further above him, above the ceiling, his ceiling, which was another person's floor, he could hear the slip slop as the woman of the apartment washed her floors. Outside he could hear the sound of traffic in the street, the honking of the horns, an occasional squeal of tyres.

In the ashtray beside the chair were mounds of cigarette butts and a pile of ash. In the park, the other day, there had just been him and Guilo walking. They had seen a group of children, but it had just been him and Guilo really. No one else. They had walked together and talked and agreed to separate and not to see each other and only to contact each other by phone, or maybe letter. It was important no longer to be seen together; that they agreed. Duccio had found it easy to say but hard to do because it meant that he now had only his anxiety and his imagination to keep him company. And his nerves had never been good.

Then he heard the tap at the door. A soft tapping, just three taps, tap, tap, tap. He rose from the chair, stood still, listened, but he didn't hear it again. But he had heard it; of that he was certain. A child, perhaps, a child too short to reach the doorbell. He rose and walked silently towards the door. He peered through the peephole and, seeing nothing, drew back and frowned. His feet shuffled on the floor as he put his eye to the eye-piece once again.

Outside in the corridor, Carlo stood to one side of the peephole, the automatic pointing into the door at a slight angle, at chest height, directly below the eye-piece. His ears strained, sifting sounds, the traffic, the clattering of refuse bins outside the backs of the apartment building . . . the shuffling of feet, just on the other side of the door . . .

Now.

Again, the automatic leapt violently in his hand, and sent a small piece of lead hurtling through the flimsy door at supersonic speed, yet it made only the softest, gentlest 'phutt' sound. Even the sound of the bullet crashing through the door panel made a noise of only negligible volume. Not so negligible and very pleasing to the assassin's ears was the sound of a body, a human body, crashing to the floor, picked up and flung backwards by the sheer energy of the bullet.

Later, weeks later, an official report of the inquest of the death of the man was to find its way via a series of unofficial channels onto Carlo's desk; a single soft-nosed bullet had shattered the victim's heart.

*   *   *

Francesca Arcalli lay on the same hard bed in the same cockroach infested room: the hotel room she had occupied now for three days, making herself a virtual prisoner, sending out for meals, and for cigarettes. When she did leave the room, it was only to venture as far as the hotel lobby where she read the morning and the evening papers, which were displayed on a table near the desk. She lay on her bed and wondered how best to approach the man from Glasgow.

Soon she could escape into a siesta. Just one more cigarette and then she would close the shutters.

The phone on the table beside her bed rang with a nerve-jangling note. She tensed, let it ring. Then reached out and picked it up.

Guilo huddled over the pay phone in the café. He watched the *carabinieri* as they swarmed about the apartment block opposite; he watched as Duccio's body was brought out on a blanket-covered stretcher. The phone rang, then it was picked up. He heard Francesca say, cautiously, 'Yes.' He identified himself and began to speak.

'. . . I don't know how but they did. I heard it on the news. I came over. It is Duccio. It could only be him . . . no, the radio didn't identify the victim, just said a shooting incident and gave Duccio's address. They're just carrying out the body now . . . no, I don't know how but they did. They must have been following him, or us. Marco was right,' Guilo said bitterly, harshly. 'It's Pietro.' He paused, then added angrily. 'Who else could it be? Francesca, you've got to get out quickly.'

In the room, she lay on the bed, staring at the ceiling. She had put the phone down five minutes earlier. For five minutes she looked up at the ceiling, following the cracks in the plaster. Then, after five minutes of complete silence she said, 'Thank you, Guilo.'

It was all she needed, just that bit of extra push.

Action, Francesca. Action.

*   *   *

Rossi cast the fishing-line and then played it with his right hand. The loch, blue-black, stretched out before him and gave way to a pine-covered hillside which in turn became heather-covered mountain, purple in the distance. The sky was blue, a wisp of cloud. It was peaceful, by the waterside. He played the line again. He enjoyed fishing, not just for the relaxation it offered, not the skill of playing a trout, but the way that it opened up a fascinating view of life in, on and above the water. Once he had watched an osprey swoop and pluck a salmon from a sea loch. There was the day he had seen a basking shark in Loch Fyne, 30 feet in length if it was an inch. Once on the shore of Loch Long, the water around him suddenly erupted into a frenzy and fish spiralled into the air and crashed seawards again; others threw themselves suicidally onto the shore. The fish were whitebait, they had been chased and finally cornered by a shoal of hungry and carnivorous mackerel.

'You ought to try this, Alistair.' Rossi played the line with his right hand and turned to where Sinclair Murray sat in a deckchair. 'It's very relaxing.'

Sinclair Murray sat with his eyes closed. He reached beside him, lifted a glass of champagne and sipped.

'Do I,' he said, between sips, 'appear to be suffering from stress and strain, Dominic? Me, comfortably established as I am in the law?'

'Not at all,' Rossi turned his attentions once again to the loch. 'It's just that I thought that persons of your ilk, the upper classes, were devoted to huntin', shootin' and fishin'.'

'Not this one, Dominic, not this one. I'm green. Are you perchance, perhaps, in the mood for some gossip?'

'The only thing green about you is your wellies. What gossip?'

Sinclair Murray struggled out of the deckchair and walked over to where Rossi stood:

'A word of warning.'

Sinclair Murray stared out over the smooth water, and enjoyed the breeze on his face. He was aware of Rossi's questioning sidelong glance, but chose not to look him in the eye.

'Yes, I think warning would be more accurate than gossip. Your junior partner, the thrusting Ms Goodchild and her recent waltz with one Detective Inspector Ballantyne did not go down well with the constabulary. She was felt to have gone well over the top.'

'Well, shock horror.' Rossi said, then paused. 'Oh, come on, she was doing her job, and she did it well, you know that, and I know that; anyway, she's a prosecutor turned defender and they always go tooth and nail after their old pals. Part of the game.'

'The general perception is that you have retired from criminal work and so you are encouraging the previously mentioned Ms Goodchild to become, and I quote, "a female Dominic Rossi".'

'Encouraging her!' Rossi flushed with anger. 'Hell's teeth, she said she wanted experience outside the criminal territory and, I repeat, outside. That's why I took her on, to help us shift the mountain of conveyancing work that we've got backing up. So along the way she proved herself to be a natural trial lawyer; you think I ought to rein in talent like that? Not likely. But since you bring up the issue, I have asked her to widen her work load.'

'I simply report, Dominic. I do not comment.'

'You . . . er . . .' Rossi sought for the right way to express a sudden suspicion. 'You weren't asked to do this . . . reporting, were you? Is this why you got me out here?'

'Well,' Sinclair Murray replied blandly, 'it was put to me that we are all part of the system and that there are relationships to be considered . . . including those with the police.'

Sinclair Murray was aware of Rossi's angry gaze, nonetheless he drove his point home. 'I'm also reliably informed that Big Jim Ballantyne, as I believe he likes to be known, is a bad enemy.'

Rossi paused, absorbing the implications of Sinclair Murray's words. He thought it was a bit like being inducted into a secret society.

'Well,' he said eventually, 'you can tell the general perception and, I quote, "get stuffed", and you can also tell it to Big Jim, as he likes to be known, Ballantyne. I'm not afraid of making enemies, Alistair, in fact I rather enjoy it.

'You enjoy it!' This time Sinclair Murray did look at Rossi.

'I guess I'm a little twisted like that; I enjoy making friends, I also enjoy making enemies. It's the way I am.'

'You're a complicated man, Dominic,' said Sinclair Murray, stepping back as the line bent suddenly.

They walked from the loch, up the forestry commission track, to where Sinclair Murray's cottage stood in a small dell, surrounded by pine trees, just beside the track, yet deep in the glen and satisfactorily remote. They walked without speaking, Rossi carrying his rod and line, Sinclair Murray carrying his hamper and deckchair.

They ate a most unsatisfying lunch of fishfingers. The two men ate in silence, a silence which was only broken by the small black and white television set switched on by Sinclair Murray, who was anxious not to miss the midday news.

'You ever hear from Doctor Kate these days?' Sinclair Murray wiped his lips delicately with a paper serviette.

'Not for a couple of months.' Rossi then paused. 'In fact, I hear through the grapevine that she's thinking of getting married.'

Sinclair Murray looked at him. Rossi shrugged. 'Well, I was upset at the time, blamed myself, went through that whole number. Now I think it was for the best, wouldn't have worked. You know what they say in Glasgow, "What's for you, will not go by you". Anyway, to change the subject, it's not that I've given up the criminal work, Alistair, it's just that . . .' Rossi stopped speaking suddenly as Sinclair Murray stood, reaching for the volume control of the television set, turning the volume up . . ..

'. . . today at Westminster,' said the voice of the newscaster. 'He was Member of Parliament for Glasgow Woodside.'

'Well, well,' said Rossi. 'I have a friend who will be excited by that news.'

'Oh?' Sinclair Murray reduced the volume and resumed his seat.

'Journalist, leftie sort of bloke, you'd hate him, I confess I don't see eye to eye with him politically, but I like him. Guy called Gerry Cowan, recently accepted by the Labour Party as their candidate for, would you believe it . . . .'

'Glasgow Woodside?'

'The one and the same. He wasn't expecting to fight an election for years.'

'Just shows,' Sinclair Murray closed his eyes. 'None of us knows what's ahead of us.'

* * *

Rossi and Sinclair Murray returned separately to Glasgow. Rossi drove straight to Cowan's flat. He had to ring the bell several times before it was answered. The door was eventually flung open and revealed a flat in a state of pandemonium. Rossi was not the only visitor, not the only visitor by far.

'Came to see if you'd heard the news,' said Rossi, stepping over the threshold, 'but I think I'm a bit late. Dare say it was a bit silly of me to think that a journalist hadn't heard the news, any news.'

'It's been like a madhouse for the past hour.' Cowan closed the door behind Rossi.

A long-haired young man stepped into the hall. 'Gerry,' he said anxiously. 'They're making all the same mistakes. We've got to . . . .'

'All right, Tommy,' Cowan replied calmly. 'I'll be back there in a minute.' He turned to Rossi. 'See them,' he said, 'See them. If that lot ever thought that they were going to have the chance of getting back Woodside this side of the general election, they'd never have let an accredited wild man like me get the nomination. Now they're trying to sort me out fast. Make me into a Socialist yuppie.'

The phone rang in the hall as Rossi said cheerfully, 'Well, looks like you've got the ethnic vote tied up already. Eleanor says those Chinese guys speak very warmly of you.' It especially amused him to think that the efforts of the reactionary Eleanor Goodchild on behalf of Mr Wong and Mr Chen might have indirectly assisted the fervently radical Cowan.

Rossi felt out of place and under-employed in Cowan's flat. He was not a political animal and there was no niche for him among the bustle and fervour. He drove home and let himself in through the front door of his house, placing the fishing tackle just inside the door, among the boots and the raincoats.

'It's got potential,' he said, 'real potential.' But inwardly he felt dissatisfied. He felt the house was a vast, lonely, soulless building.

It was odd, he thought, that the good fortune of a

friend should make him feel depressed. He was pleased for Gerry, but Gerry's good fortune just served to bring home to him the uncertain direction of his own life. It was odd. The success of an adversary would galvanise him into action. The success of a friend had strangely the opposite effect.

He wandered down the hallway of the house and stepped into the kitchen. He filled the kettle to make a cup of coffee and, while the kettle was heating up, he edged casually to the other side of the table and glanced out of the window.

His heart missed a beat.

His mouth opened slightly. He placed his fingertips gently on the glass. He dared not believe what he saw. The child's swing had always been there, to the left of the kitchen. Its eventual removal was on the long list of 'jobs to be done' which Rossi occasionally rearranged to give himself the illusion of making headway. Beside the swing were two suitcases which had certainly not always been there. On the swing, moving gently backwards and forwards, with her back to the house gazing towards the city, was a woman. Rossi, not unreasonably, took her to be the owner of the suitcases.

The woman was Francesca Arcalli.

Rossi continued to stare at Francesca who still sat on the swing, gazing out across the city, completely unaware of his presence. He opened the rear door of the house and she turned at the sound of the drawing of the bolt, smiling warmly at him.

He stood at the edge of the lawn, excitement rising uncontrollably in his chest. He stepped towards her, gathering pace as he did so. She stood and faced him with open, outstretched arms.

Rossi was running when he reached her; he stopped, pulling her to him, burying his head into her shoulder, delighting as her arms clasped him tightly to her. He laughed unashamedly, laughed with undisguised joy at her presence. They kissed, then separated, gasping for breath, and kissed again. He laughed aloud, shaking his head, not daring to allow himself to believe that he held her in his arms.

'God,' he said, 'you don't realise how much . . . I think that I'm going to wake up any minute . . . .'

'Me too, Dominic.'

'What are you doing here?' He laughed again with sheer delight.

'I just had to come and see you . . . I can't explain it any better than that . . . you don't mind, do you?'

'Mind . . . mind . . ,' he held her tightly, thrilling to the touch of her body as he held her close. 'Of course I don't mind! Welcome to Glasgow!'

'You don't know how glad I am to be here,' Francesca answered and clung to him as if to a rock in a raging sea.

Chapter 4

FATHER PIETRO came across the photograph again. It was something he did from time to time, always when searching for something, never deliberately seeking out the battered old print. On this occasion, a Sunday morning, fumbling with his cassock he had noticed a button was missing. He had searched quickly for a needle and thread as the church bells began to toll over Cocullo, perched high, in the mountains, among the forests and the rarified air. He had opened a drawer in the small desk in his room, rummaged for a needle and thread, and come upon the photograph. He had not seen it for, how long now, six months, perhaps longer. He sat and studied it. It was part of his past, not a period that he was proud of, but he believed that what he did in those days, ten years ago, was just. He believed that the ends had justified the means and it was as simple as that.

They had all believed that.

All of them, here in this photograph; Marco, had believed, Guilio, had believed, Duccio and Guiseppe. All had shared a common cause . . . as had Francesca. The others, he found came to mind once a week, once a month, but he found that he thought of Francesca daily. Even after all these years. He did not think of her constantly, or obsessively, his parish filled his mind with work. But on those odd occasions when his mind was not occupied, walking across the square of Cocullo, riding his motor cycle out to visit a distant parishioner, then it would be the memory of Francesca which would flood into his mind and occupy the void.

He wondered what had become of them? Francesca, he had heard, had returned to her parents' villa, a move which had surprised him at the time and which still saddened him. Guiseppe had become a taxi-driver in Rome, whether he still was, the priest did not know.

The bell continued to toll. Father Pietro placed the photograph at the rear of the drawer. He closed the drawer and stood, turning, to leave the room. The button could wait.

*   *   *

In the garden of a house, the walled, high-gated garden of a Roman suburb, a man sat on a bench. He was a portly, well-set man, in slacks, sandals and a dressing-gown. On the table in front of him was a tall, silver coffee pot, a cup and saucer. On the bench beside him were the Sunday newspapers. He closed one newspaper and reached for another; as he did so, his eye was caught by movement to his right. He turned. He saw his aide standing with another man. The second man was well-dressed, trim, in early middle age. He wore a puzzled, yet serious expression. The aide retreated into the house and the man stepped onto the lawn, carrying a slender paper file.

'Minister?' he said, as he approached the garden bench, remaining at a respectful distance.

'Ah, Cristaldi,' replied the seated man, feigning surprise at Cristaldi's sudden appearance. 'I do apologise to you for asking you here on a Sunday morning, in your free time.'

'As a senior member of the *carabinieri*, I regard my time as belonging to the State, Minister.'

The Minister nodded and smiled. 'Well, I respect your dedication and your commitment, Cristaldi, it does not go unnoticed. I will not keep you longer than necessary.' He patted the newspapers which lay beside him, throwing up a glare in the mid-morning sun. 'I am concerned about these murders, the newspapers are suggesting a link. You know the ones to which I am referring; the taxi-driver in the middle of the city in the middle of the day; the man outside the café also in the middle of the day; the man shot through the front door of his flat . . . .'

'I have read the newspapers, Minister. I am aware of the murders.'

'Have you read today's papers?'

'Not yet, Minister.'

'Do so, please, Cristaldi, then you'll see why I have been advised by those who know of such things that you are the man to speak to.' The Minister reached forward and lifted the coffee pot as if to weigh its contents. 'Coffee?' he asked.

'No thank you, Minister.' Cristaldi knew the answer that the Minister wanted to hear. He did not need a policeman's eye to see the caked staining of the cup, evidence of the Minister's coffee intake that morning, nor did he need to be told that if he wanted coffee then a second cup would have to be sent for with all the inconvenience and disruption that would necessitate. But the invitation had to be extended, as Cristaldi knew, and, as he also knew, it had to be politely declined. The game over, the interview could proceed.

'I hear rumours,' the Minister continued. 'Rumours that these killings are politically linked. And as Internal Security is my responsibility, then I'd prefer to be given the facts as you might know them, before I am asked questions about the rumours. The newspapers have already commented that the m.o. is that of a trained and a highly skilled assassin and that adds weight to the rumour that the killings are politically linked. I would like to be made aware of what is going on. Do you hear me?'

'We do know a little, Minister.' Cristaldi replied,

'We know that those three deceased had a common past. In fact, I anticipated the reason for you asking me to attend your home this morning.' He handed the Minister the file. 'That is the sum total of our findings at the present. It isn't much, I concede, but I'm afraid the rest is speculation.'

'I don't like speculation, Cristaldi.' The Minister took the file. 'There's too much speculation. Just find the man or woman who is behind this, who is responsible, and do it fast.'

'We're doing all we can.' Cristaldi's attempt to placate the Minister sounded all too meek, even to his own ears. 'The file is all classified information, Sir.'

'You don't have to tell me that.' The Minister, once warm and affable, was now becoming testy. 'Besides, I have a sufficiently high security clearance.' He paused. 'I have a theory, a theory of my own, Cristaldi. Have you considered revenge as a possible motive?'

'Revenge, Minister?' Cristaldi replied, feeling the sun burning the right side of his head. He half-closed his eyes against the glare. 'I don't understand, Sir.'

'It's not so difficult to understand, Cristaldi. I know that police officers are not noted for their brain power, but surely you see the possibility of a revenge attack. These, these, victims . . .' he struck at the newspapers with the back of his hand, 'you said they had something, as yet undetermined, in common. So they damaged someone, a relative, something like that, they introduced an adolescent to hard drugs, the drugs killed him, so the parent or brother or sister, is hunting them down and killing them. It's as simple as that.'

'Minister,' Cristaldi shrugged. 'It's an interesting theory, a very interesting theory – we should consider that.'

The Minister laughed, reached up and clasped Cristaldi by the arm. Affable, then testy then affable, all in the space of thirty seconds. Cristaldi pitied anyone who had to work with the Minister. Still more, he pitied anyone who had to live with him.

'Make sure that you keep me informed, Cristaldi. I don't like to be kept in the dark.'

'Of course, Minister.' Cristaldi gave a slight, deferential nod.

'I'm sorry, once again, I'm sorry to have disturbed your Sunday morning.'

'As my time is the State's then . . . well, Sunday is also just another working day. I am not at all unhappy.'

'Good man.' The Minister offered his hand. 'So, we'll have some results soon?'

'I have my best man on the job.' Cristaldi shook the Minister's hand.

'Oh, who?'

'Carlo Alphonsi, Minister.'

'Carlo Alphonsi, it's a name I haven't heard before.'

'He's very, very good, Minister. Very good indeed.'

Cristaldi drove from the Minister's house into central Rome. He parked his car in the front of the building and ran up the entrance steps two at a time, acknowledging the salute of the duty *carabiniere* as he swept past the man. He walked down the corridor, his footfall echoing in the silent hallway. He entered his office and sat at the desk, swivelling the chair towards a computer console with a monitoring screen. Cristaldi glanced out of the tall window of his office into the courtyard below and then turned his attention once again to the computer. He tapped the keyboard and studied the terminal. 'Information restricted' glared in green on the screen. Cristaldi tapped a five-digit access code. The sign vanished. He tapped the keyboard again and sat back as a file index flashed onto the screen. He read the list of names with satisfaction: Guiseppe, the taxi-driver; Marco and Duccio, neither of whom seemed to have amounted to anything in life, particularly the tragic Duccio, penniless in his small dingy flat situated in that part of Rome where the tourists are dissuaded from visiting.

So, now it was three down, three to go. Any order will do, so long as the job is done, there's no rush, no time pressure. Cold dishes can be eaten slowly, just as slowly as one likes. So who or what should he savour next?

He decided he would savour the woman. He smiled a thin smile as he leant forward and ran the cursor down to the woman's name. He punched the keyboard and then leaned back in his chair and digested the known facts about Francesca Arcalli, aged thirty-two years, of Villa Arcalli, Rome.

* * *

Francesca Arcalli stirred and woke. In the distance she heard church bells ringing and, nearer at hand, she heard the soft rumble of the traffic on the motorway, light traffic as befitted a Sunday morning. It was the traffic that had awakened her, not the bells. Then she started. The room was unfamiliar, the bed and the sheets felt and smelt unfamiliar.

She shut her eyes as she relaxed from the brief and sudden flood of panic. It all came back, the flight from Ciampino to Gatwick, the clumsy journey from Gatwick to Heathrow, train and then underground train, the British Airways shuttle. She recalled the taxi-driver who had taken her from Glasgow airport to Dominic's address and who had insisted on calling her 'hen'. In the back of the taxi, she had fumbled for her Italian/English dictionary; 'hen' meant nothing but 'gallina', a chicken. There was no alternative meaning. She replaced the dictionary in her handbag and glanced at a drab housing estate, grey in the rain. It was a strange term of endearment. Even worse, she thought, than being called 'duck', which she found meant 'abbassare la testa', by the ticket collector at Victoria Station in London. The taxi had deposited her outside a rambling Victorian mansion; it was not the Villa Arcalli, but nonetheless she was not unimpressed. The rain had eased off as she walked up to the front door and rang the doorbell, then she had knocked. Eventually, she found her way to the rear of the house and awaited the homecoming of Dominic Rossi. And that night, his touch was just as gentle as she had remembered his touch being in Sorrento..

The entire day flooded back to her in a matter of seconds. She sighed contentedly and stretched her slender limbs. Here she was safe; at least for the time being.

'Buongiorno. Sleep well?' She turned. Dominic Rossi stood at the side of the bed, dressing-gown, stubble chin, ruffled hair and a mug of coffee in each hand.

She stirred again, 'I'll let you know when I wake up.' She was still sleepy but affected a greater degree of sleepiness than she felt. She wanted him to believe that she was utterly relaxed and secure in his bed. 'What time is it?' she added, smiling as she spoke. 'I feel I've slept for a year. A hundred years.'

'Half-past ten.' Rossi sat down on the edge of the

bed, leaned across her and placed the mug on the cabinet beside her. 'Drink this as quickly as you can,' he said, returning her smile. 'I've got breakfast on the go and there's a heavy day ahead of us.'

'Doing what?' Francesca levered herself into a sitting position and tucked her knees up under her chin. She reached for the mug of steaming coffee.

'Doing Glasgow,' replied Dominic, standing. 'City of Culture, and,' he added, 'if you behave yourself and make all the right appreciative noises and admire all the right things, there's a special treat tonight.'

Francesca leaned back in the bed, making no attempt to conceal herself as the sheets slid down. She raised an eyebrow, questioningly.

'A tour of the local low-life,' continued Rossi by means of explanation. 'It will be educational, not to mention cultural in its own way. I mean, really cultural in its own right.'

He took her to the Burrell Collection and the Cathedral. They lunched in town and on they went to the Art Gallery and Museum. By early evening, she was sitting in the back of Rossi's car. Rossi was at the wheel and beside Rossi was the man who had taken her seat, a small but solid-looking man in a flat cap, a man whom Rossi had introduced as Benny MacLawrie. They had driven from the city centre to the east of Glasgow.

It was a Glasgow she didn't know existed. The narrow streets of tenements reminded her of Milan. Concrete and glass highrises sprang up from the rubble of a cleared site, mounds of refuse piled up on wasteground. It was a Glasgow of pale-faced children running in the street, of large women, of small men who swayed drunkenly, of dogs which roamed in packs. This, she felt, was close to the image that the world has of Glasgow. Rossi had parked the car across the road from a small stone-built chapel. Five minutes after they arrived, a small group of people began to file out of the door. The man in the front passenger seat took out a packet of cigarettes, offering it to Francesca and then to Rossi; both declined. MacLawrie lit his cigarette as they watched the congregation leave the chapel.

'Devout, is he?' Rossi asked. 'I mean, this nephew of yours, is he a good Catholic?'

Benny MacLawrie shook his head. 'No,' he said, exhaling smoke in a long plume. 'It's the old situation. His mother, my sister, would kick seven bells out of him if he didn't show willing. He found by trial and error that the 6.00 p.m. mass at St Marie's here is the shortest in the east end. So he puts in an appearance here, keeps his ma happy.'

'I see,' Rossi smiled. 'So, the junior member of the notorious MacLawrie clan is afraid of his mother. So many hard men seem to be frightened of mother. I always find that a little odd.'

'Just a minute,' MacLawrie's voice hardened. 'She's a big woman, is my sister; she'd make four of me . . . it's no shame for a boy to be frightened of his mother . . . Wait. Here, that's him coming out now.'

Benny MacLawrie fumbled with the door handle, got out of the car clumsily and walked across to the chapel. Francesca and Rossi watched as he approached a slightly built teenager, a boy of about seventeen, thought Rossi, emaciated with a pinched face and shabbily dressed in casual clothing.

'Promised you the local low-life, didn't I?' Rossi turned to Francesca and grinned as he spoke. 'Well, this is it.' Francesca returned the smile.

'Where are we going now, Dominic?' she asked, as MacLawrie and his nephew walked towards the car.

Rossi shrugged, 'We'll find a quiet pub,' he said. 'It's as good as anywhere.'

They went to a corner pub in Partick, close to the bottom of Byres Road. It was Sunday evening, quiet, a few people in. Music played and a huge television set sat high on the wall to the left of the bar with the sound turned down. The building was old, but to Francesca's professional eye it seemed to have been recently refurbished. There was a red carpet on the floor, the chairs were simple on small tubular frames, with minimal upholstery. The sides of the bar were of polished wooden panelling, with photographs and drawings of men in boxing shorts and gloves. It was not a young person's pub, which pleased Francesca. Most of the people in the pub seemed to be middle-aged or elderly. They were well dressed. It was the same in Italy; she had noticed that the people the British call 'working class' dress up to go out, the 'middle classes' dress down. The bar itself was tended by two young women in white blouses and black skirts.

'So tell Mr Rossi what happened, Gerard.' Ben MacLawrie nudged Gerard who sat, or rather slouched, opposite Francesca. She thought him resentful, as if he felt that he had been dealt some injustice in life. She turned her attention to him, awaiting his reply.

'On you go,' said MacLawrie, 'tell him, just like you told me.'

'What's the point?' Gerard replied, sarcastically, avoiding eye contact with anybody; he looked at the ashtray on the table as he spoke. 'I mean, they've had my cards marked for years. Give *me* a break, some chance.'

'Have the police done you before?' Rossi asked him. Gerard nodded.

'Aye,' he said, sullenly.

'What do you call it?' MacLawrie turned to Rossi, 'Petty theft, nothing major, fines, probation he got, that's all.'

'I see,' Rossi nodded. 'Look Gerard,' he said, a hard

edge creeping into his voice. 'It's no skin off my nose, none at all. So if you want to sit there and play the martyr, that's up to you. But your uncle here persuaded me to come and meet you. I've come out of my way to meet you, my ladyfriend here has come out of her way, to meet you. So that's what we are doing, for another five seconds or thereabouts.' Rossi sipped his drink. 'In other words, it's make your mind up time. Either help yourself and keep us here or play games alone.'

Gerard lifted his pint and scowled into it. He drank deeply and put the glass down hard on the table. Benny MacLawrie kicked him. Gerard jumped angrily.

'Tell the man while you can, Gerard,' said MacLawrie, growling at his nephew.

'It's dead simple,' Gerard said at length. 'Simple, easy to understand. I was supposed to meet this guy I know, right? We were going for a drink and he turns up driving this van. He says that he's got a loan of it, off his boss, he says, for the night.' He drank more beer. 'So, I get in, don't I, and off we go for a wee run. Then we get stopped by the cops because the rear lights aren't working and the next thing I know we're both in the cells.'

'Because,' said Rossi, 'as your uncle told me, there's eighteen thousand quid in notes stuffed in a polybag underneath the seat.'

'So what!' Gerard spat the words. 'It's a free country, isn't it? I mean, it's supposed to be! How was I to know it was there, how am I supposed to know where Mickey got the money? Or how he got it.'

'Look', said Ben MacLawrie, somewhat impatiently, 'we, and particularly Mr Rossi, are trying to help you. It's not our fault you got lifted, it's not our fault you've been charged with theft which you had nothing to do with, so stop taking it out on us will you? Start helping us to help you.'

'Thanks, but it'll blow over,' he spoke defiantly and drained his glass. 'I mean, it's just not worth bothering about. You'll see. I mean, you'll see if I'm wrong.' He stood. 'It was good of you to put yourself out for me, Mr Rossi. But I'll handle this myself.' Gerard walked from the table and weaved his way across the carpet to the door, stepping back as he reached the door to allow a drunk to stagger inside.

'It's his way of saying that he wants help, Mr Rossi,' Ben MacLawrie explained. 'He's a strange lad at times, doesn't want to appear weak. So he says that he can do it alone, that he doesn't need help, but in a day or two he'll contact you.'

'Strange, as you say,' said Rossi, watching the two young women behind the bar politely, but firmly, refuse to serve the drunk.

'On your way, John,' said one. She opened the hinged section of the bar, walked up to the drunk and led him by the hand, like a child, across the floor and out of the bar.

'The other boy,' said Rossi, 'Mickey . . . somebody.'

'Conner,' said MacLawrie sipping his whisky. 'Michael Conner. Some family, always in bother. I never did like the idea of our Gerard teaming up with him. My sister liked it even less.'

'I see, so this Mickey Conner, has he got himself a lawyer? I'd like to talk to him.'

'Yes, he has,' said MacLawrie, 'he's asked that guy in the shopping precinct, I mean the guy whose office is in the shopping precinct, to represent him. Fellow by the name of Flanagan. Do you know him?'

'Tom Flanagan?' Rossi nodded and smiled. 'Yes, I know Tom Flanagan.'

MacLawrie turned to Francesca, 'Sorry about all this . . .' he broke off as a woman screamed outside. The pub fell silent and then conversation resumed. 'Not even a Friday as well,' he said, as two men left the bar to investigate. 'Yes, I'm sorry about all this, Miss – it's not what I'd call a holiday.'

'No, please, don't be sorry, Mr MacLawrie. It's interesting for me, this is very interesting.'

'I don't get away much myself, you know. I went to Benidorm once. Have you been there, it's really nice . . .'

MacLawrie broke off as one of the men who had

left the bar to investigate the scream rushed in, shouting, 'Get an ambulance, quick.' The girl who had taken the drunk outside snatched up the phone behind the bar.

'. . . I preferred North Africa,' said MacLawrie.

'. . . where the locks are old-fashioned,' Rossi grinned but as he did so he watched the man who had shouted for the ambulance approach their table.

The man stood over their table. 'That boy, who was sitting with you, just a minute ago . . .'

'Aye?' said MacLawrie, a worried look on his face. 'He's my nephew.'

'I think you'd better come outside, Jim,' said the man.

MacLawrie shot to his feet and left the bar followed by Rossi. Picking up her bag, Francesca wasn't far behind.

Outside, darkness had fallen. She watched Rossi and MacLawrie run to where a crowd was gathering on the pavement. She increased her speed. She saw Rossi kneel down next to a dark mound which rested in the gutter; as she approached he got up and came towards her. He stopped her moving further forward, further towards the dark mound. In the distance, she heard the ambulance. She looked at the shape in the gutter and the shape became a human. More than that, it became Gerard, who just minutes earlier had been scowling into his pint and who had stood up angrily saying that it would blow over, and anyway he could handle it.

Rossi drove her home. Not a word passed between them during the journey. They entered his house and walked into the living-room. Francesca sat on the sofa, hunched up, tense, yet distant. Rossi poured two brandies. He handed one to her; she took it gratefully.

'I'm sorry,' he said.

'It's not your fault,' she said, sipping the drink. 'Oh, I need this.'

'I'm sorry that you had to have that experience.'

'I've seen things like that before, Dominic. I haven't been wrapped in cotton wool all my life.'

'Nonetheless, . . .' Rossi sat beside her and put his arm round her, 'it's an experience you could have done without. It's an experience we could both have done without.'

Francesca nodded. 'To think that just a minute earlier he was drinking and talking with us . . .'

Rossi nodded. 'I know,' he said. 'You never know the minute, do you? None of us know the minute . . .'

Later, much later, in the middle of the night, in bed, something made him wake up. He turned over and found that he was alone. Francesca had slipped away. He eased himself out of bed and put on a dressing-gown. He went downstairs and found

Francesca in the living-room, sitting in front of the fire with a blanket around her shoulders. She looked up and smiled as he came in.

'Bad dreams,' she said, by way of explanation. Rossi nodded, forced a smile and turned to go back upstairs. He frowned as he walked away. Francesca's explanation posed more questions than it answered. It was not just Gerard's accident that was stopping her from sleeping. There was more to it than that.

Chapter 5

MONDAY MORNING DAWNED grey and overcast. Rossi got up as gently as he could, trying not to disturb the slumbering Francesca. He washed, then dressed outside the bedroom and ate a hasty breakfast in the kitchen. He picked the phone off the wall and dialled his office.

'Shona,' he said, chewing a slice of toast, 'Dominic . . . I'm going to be late in this morning. I'm going out to see Tom Flanagan. . . . No, he's a solicitor . . . has an office in Drumchapel. . . . If I'm needed urgently, you can contact me there . . . sorry, I don't have it to hand, but it'll doubtless be in the Yellow Pages . . . bye.'

Rossi abandoned a mug of coffee, left his house and drove out to Drumchapel.

Drumchapel sprawled over three hills on the western edge of the city, mainly low-rise tenement dwellings, with one or two high-rise developments. It was the second largest housing scheme in the city in terms of population and the largest in the city in terms of area. Fifty to sixty per cent of the working population were unemployed; there was a major drug problem, a major alcohol problem, a significant number of the houses were rotten with damp. It was where Tom Flanagan had chosen to set up his law firm.

Rossi parked his car close to the shopping precinct and walked across the litter-strewn 'piazza'. He entered what, to all appearances, seemed to be an empty shop. What had been the front of a shop was now a waiting-room. Three people sat on chairs, leafing through magazines. On the wall were welfare rights posters and a large poster of Austria, just, Rossi assumed, for decoration. As Rossi entered, the door to the inner office opened, and Tom Flanagan showed a middle-aged woman out.

'Don't forget,' said Flanagan, 'it's vital that you tell the social worker to get in touch with me as soon as she can.'

'All right, Mr Flanagan,' said the woman. Flanagan turned to Rossi and nodded in recognition. 'Are you coming in?' he said politely.

Rossi passed the woman and entered Flanagan's office. Flanagan was dressed casually, in corduroys and a sweatshirt on which was printed 'The Law is an Ass'.

'I always preferred the notion that the law is a *derrière*,' said Rossi, entering the office which was as shabby as Flanagan was himself.

'This is the other side of justice, Mr Rossi,' said Flanagan, noticing Rossi's disapproving look. 'Please take a seat. I expect your office is a bit better than this.' Rossi sat down in the hard chair in front of Flanagan's desk.

'Well, everybody has to start somewhere, Tom, and I take my hat off to you for practising what you preach.'

'Well, point one, Mr Rossi, I'm not starting, I'm staying here.' Flanagan paused. 'Practising what I preach – do you remember me, then?'

'Certainly, Tom,' said Rossi, as Flanagan sat behind his desk. 'I remember you all right, Tom Flanagan. You always sat next to that girl with the red hair, and you always asked the most awkward questions.'

Flanagan raised his eyebrows. 'Well, I'm flattered, Mr Rossi. Are you still doing those seminars?'

Rossi shook his head. 'No, in fact I haven't done them for quite a while now. I used to enjoy them, though. Good fun, kept me sharp!'

'Good fun!' Flanagan laughed. 'Getting torn into by a bunch of Bolshie final year law students?'

'You weren't all bolshie.'

'More's the pity, if you ask me. You know, I could do with some help around here; the work's backing up. I don't suppose you fancy chucking up your big plush office and getting back to the sharp end?'

'It's the sharp end I want to speak to you about – Gerard MacLawrie.'

'Oh yes,' Flanagan said, nodding his head. 'The

Gerard and Mickey show. Eighteen grand underneath the passenger seat. Gerard's been a bad boy.' Flanagan paused. 'I really didn't think that this was your kind of case, a bit down market for you, isn't it, Mr Rossi?'

Rossi didn't care for the jibe, a bit cheap, he thought, but he let it ride. 'That's not what Gerard says,' he said, 'about being the bad guy, I mean.'

'Well, as the lady once said, he would, wouldn't he?' Tom Flanagan sat forward. 'Look, Mr Rossi. I've known the Conners for years and they're a rough squad of a family. You know, Mrs Average might brag about the good degree her son's just won; well, Mrs Conner would brag about the ten-year stretch one of her happy brood has just been sent down for. Some family, the Conners, believe me; but Michael's different, he really is.'

'So, what's his story?'

'As it was relayed to me, it's that your boy, Gerard MacLawrie, phoned Mickey and asked him to borrow the van and meet him. So Gerard duly shows up; he's got the bag with the loot and says that he's looking after it for a friend. Shortly after that, they were stopped by the boys in blue.'

'Well,' said Rossi, 'one of them is lying.'

'Looks that way. But your client is the one with the tallest story, not mine.'

'My client is also in the Western Infirmary. Intensive care.'

'Oh,' said Flanagan. 'I'm sorry to hear that. What happened?'

'Hit-and-run. Don't suppose you'd know where your client was at about nine o'clock last night?'

'No, I don't. I also can't see Michael Conner pulling a stunt like that. Any of his brothers, yes, but not Mickey.'

'Well, I dare say that truth will out in good time. It always does.'

'No, it doesn't,' said Flanagan firmly. 'Don't kid yourself, Mr Rossi.'

*   *   *

Rossi wasn't prepared for the sight which met him and Flanagan at the hospital. With hindsight he knew that he should have expected it, considering the mess that the car had made of Gerard MacLawrie. The plain truth of it was that for him hospitals meant cure. They didn't mean death.

As they entered the electronically controlled doors of the Western Infirmary, Flanagan asked what he considered a fatuous question – 'No description of the car?'

'Sure,' said Rossi, angrily, sarcastically. 'Black Jag, green BMW, even a red Lada with a clockwork key in the back. I mean, take your pick.'

'I didn't think it was such a stupid question,' Flanagan protested, stung by Rossi's shortness. 'It seems a sensible one to me. Obvious as well.'

They entered the waiting area where people sat quietly locked in their thoughts. Some nursed obvious injuries; an arm in a sling, a foot resting on a stool. Some had no obvious injuries but looked deeply worried, about themselves, about a loved one.

'If there had been a description, I would have told you . . .' His voice trailed off. In the far corner of the room, under the 'No Smoking' sign, a slim-built man comforted a well-built woman. The slim-built man was Benny MacLawrie, who preferred Tunisia to Benidorm. The large woman who wept uncontrollably could only be his sister, mother of Gerard. Further, Rossi reasoned, Gerard's mother could only be in floods of tears for one reason and one reason only.

Then, in an instant, hospitals ceased to mean cure. Rossi and Flanagan stopped and stood still, not wanting to approach, not wanting to turn and walk away.

'Looks like we're too late,' said Rossi. 'I didn't think . . .' He broke off as the bulk and anger of Chief Inspector McManus brushed against him and then recognised Rossi and Flanagan.

McManus snarled at Flanagan, 'God help your boy when we pick him up.'

'What do you mean, Mr McManus?' said Flanagan,

with a coolness and self-possession which surprised and also impressed Rossi.

McManus breathed deeply. 'By the look of it, Mr Flanagan,' he said, 'Micky Conner has done a runner and Gerard MacLawrie's toes are pointing up the way, skywards, and I can add two and two. I didn't get where I am by having nothing but steam between my ears.' McManus turned to Rossi. 'So,' he said interrogatively, 'what's your interest in this, Mr Rossi?'

Rossi shrugged. 'Academic now, I guess.'

'What's that supposed to mean?'

'Well, dead men may tell tales, but they pay no fees,' said Rossi, pointedly, politely. 'In a nutshell, it means I'm off the case, Chief Inspector McManus, unlike your good self who will doubtless plod on regardless until you have felt the collar of the felon what did this here dastardly deed.'

'You know something,' McManus looked at Rossi, then at Flanagan and again at Rossi. 'I hate lawyers. Hate them. If you knew of the man hours we put in to nail some little ned and people like you, with your fat fees, get him off on some technicality, like the wrong address on the warrant. . .'

'It's an important point,' said Rossi, recalling a personal victory.

'It may well be, Mr Rossi, but have you considered the effect of your legal technicalities in the real world, a known thief or violent criminal walks, grinning from ear to ear. Don't explain your attitude to me, I get my salary at the end of the month, try explaining it to the victims of the crime, or the relatives of a murdered man, or a raped girl. Try looking them in the eye while boasting about your technicalities.'

Detective Inspector Ballantyne entered the room. McManus nodded at him, glared at Rossi and Flanagan for a further second or two, and then walked angrily away to join Ballantyne.

'You succeeded in rattling his cage,' said Flanagan.

'Listen,' said Rossi, 'I've known him a long time and believe me, he never recovered from the time when he was lying in his cot and his big sister used to poke him with a stick. I think we'd better go and say something to Mrs MacLawrie by way of condolence, then leave quickly and diplomatically.'

*   *   *

Rossi put his arm round Francesca. 'That's the Sheriff Court,' he said, pointing to the large concrete building on the south bank of the Clyde. 'It's the busiest court in Europe and the most modern. Did you know that it's blast-proof?'

'Blast-proof?' Francesca looked at him. The light wind tugged at her hair and, immediately behind her, the ensign of the boat flapped in the breeze.

'Well, we live in troubled times,' Rossi explained. 'Terrorism has to be taken seriously.'

A look flashed across Francesca's eyes. It was there an instant and then gone, but it was there and Rossi saw it. The word terrorism meant something to her. Had she been a victim? – those parts of her life which she had not mentioned. He decided not to pry. She would tell him in her own time.

'Blast-proof. You see, if a bomb explodes, people are damaged either by shrapnel or by the blast, if they are not killed outright. Shrapnel can be dug out of you, bones can be mended, but the long-term disabling damage is done by the blast. It can cause internal injuries, especially to the respiratory system.'

'I see,' she said, a little falsely he thought, as if somehow she knew already.

'So, the roof of each courtroom and the corridors are false, just lightweight perspex or cardboard squares; they "give" in the event of an explosion, so that the blast is dissipated upwards, rather than being contained in a small, solidly built room.'

'How interesting,' she acknowledged.

'For the same reason, the foyer is a wide, open space in both dimensions. It's an open area from one end of the building to the other and from the floor to the roof proper, about 200 feet high. The cells are in the basement. In the old court, they were at the top of the building. Anyway, that's the shop floor, the factory, that's where we all play our little games with the law.'

114

'You don't have much respect for the law, do you,' she said as the pleasure boat slipped its mooring on the north bank and turned in a wide circle to begin its evening cruise down the Clyde.

It had not been a particularly productive day for Rossi, but he had managed to spend more time with Francesca than he had anticipated. The day had started badly with the death of Gerard MacLawrie. It had put him off work, he just couldn't concentrate. He drove home, collected Francesca, drove her into town, showed her his office, introduced her to his colleagues. It had also enabled him to show his face and he had been pleased to see Eleanor apparently coming up with the goods for the potentially valuable Chinese clients. After lunch, he and Francesca had strolled about Glasgow as he pointed out the City's vast wealth of Victorian architecture.

'It reminds me of Milan', she had said.

'It's actually twinned with Turin', he told her 'and lately Rostov in the USSR.'

In the early evening, they had taken the cruise down the water. It was a blustery day, but not uncomfortably so and they sat at the rear of the boat in the open, the glass-cased interior attracted mothers and their children and young women, in pairs.

Rossi pursed his lips, 'Well, they're using lawyers instead of rats in laboratory experiments now, have you heard that?'

'No,' she laughed.

'One, there's more of them. Lawyers, I mean. And, two, the lab technicians just don't get so fond of them. They take to rats better. And three, there are some things that a rat just will not do.'

Francesca hugged his arm, laughed again and kissed his cheek.

'I'm not saying there aren't a lot of bad guys about,' Rossi continued, allowing a note of seriousness to creep into his voice, 'but most of the ordinary people who get into trouble with the law, well, they're victims. It seems to me that society is organised to keep them down, keep them in their boxes. And the law is part of that organisation.' He paused and smiled. 'Sorry, this was meant to be a pleasure trip. Not a lecture tour.'

'It's all right.' She leant against him, resting her head on his shoulder. ' Have you made up your mind yet? About becoming an advocate, I mean?'

'Just about,' he sighed, 'the trouble is that I keep getting distracted by. . .' He pulled her to him. 'Women keep turning up on my doorstep. That kind of thing.'

'I didn't turn up on your doorstep,' she said, 'I waited dutifully on the swing until the man of the house returned.'

'So glad you came,' he said. 'Really. See that big boat there?'

116

'The *Tuxedo Princess?*' she said, reading the sign.

'It's the latest addition to Glasgow's booming, revitalised night-life, it's permanently moored, got everything, restaurant, discos, everything. If you're into that sort of thing.'

'I'm not that old,' she dug him in the ribs. 'Besides, I think I could, what is the expression you use, let down my hair tonight?'

He nodded and smiled. 'Right, you're on. *Tuxedo Princess*, here we come.'

They dined in town, had a cocktail at Charlie Parker's and jumped a taxi to the *Princess*. Rossi took Francesca to the upstairs disco – it was smaller, more intimate. He thought she danced well, very fluid in her movements. She had everything, this woman. He enjoyed the admiring glances of other men as she turned in the strobe lights. He enjoyed being seen with her. The music finished and they fell into each other's arms; Rossi's heart was thumping, beads of sweat dripped from his brow.

'Drink?' he said.

She nodded. He took her hand and guided her across the floor past the disc jockey and the music console. He noted that the record players on the console were suspended from the deck above by thin chains. He walked up to the bar which stood behind and to the left of the disc jockey's console. The lights of the south bank were visible through the portholes.

He edged and elbowed his way to the front of the bar and stood trying to catch the attention of one of the barmen. Some hope, both lads were run off their feet.

'Well, well,' shouted a voice in Rossi's ear above the music, 'fancy meeting you here.'

Rossi turned and, for the second time that day, looked into the uncompromising face of Detective Inspector Ballantyne. 'Glasgow can be a very small city.'

'Oh,' Rossi shouted back, 'every so often, I disguise myself and go out among the common people. Lawyers at play, you know. So what's your excuse, CID acting cops at play?'

'Just a quiet drink,' said Ballantyne, with forced amiability, 'a quiet drink with a wee villain who's got some stories about bigger ones.'

The barman brought two drinks for Ballantyne who tossed a five-pound note onto the counter.

'Some place for a quiet drink,' said Rossi and then quickly to the barman, 'G & T, please.'

'Sorry,' the barman shook his head. 'Guy at the end's been waiting for long enough.'

'It's as good as any,' said Ballantyne, sipping one of the drinks. 'Any sign of Mickey Conner turning up?'

Rossi shook his head. 'Ask Tom Flanagan, not me.'

'You're right,' said Ballantyne, forcing a smile. The barman returned, placed Ballantyne's change and till receipt on the bar and was gone again, no doubt, thought Rossi to serve the guy who had been waiting for long enough. Ballantyne pocketed his change and carefully placed the receipt in his wallet.

'You know, Mr Rossi. You know what I think?'

'What do you think?'

'I think that your mate, Mr Flanagan, has got a good idea where his client is and if I find out that he does, then I'm going to nail his hide to the wall alongside Mickey Conner's. Two of them hanging there, side by side, won't that make a pretty picture.' He touched the imaginary brim of an imaginary helmet, 'Evening all,' he said, picking up the drinks and elbowing his way through the crush.

Francesca and Rossi stared after him.

'You know,' said Rossi, shouting above the din, 'something's going down. I don't know what, but he knows something. And you don't come here as a cop to talk to villains. Who does he think he's kidding?'

Francesca shrugged. 'Leave it for tomorrow,' she said. '*Domani.*'

Rossi nodded and managed to catch the attention of a barman.

'*Domani,*' he agreed. 'G and T and whisky and American Dry,' he shouted.

*   *   *

'Easterhouse,' said Rossi, as he drew the car to a halt against the kerb, in answer to Francesca's question.

119

'Easterhouse is what they call this place. And no, the name has no Christian significance, it's just Scottish for east. Easter for east, wester for west. Edinburgh has a housing scheme called Westerhailes.'

'I see,' she surveyed the scheme in the fading light, low-rise tenemental buildings, fairly new, she thought, maybe twenty years old, again similar to Milan. Narrow streets. She had noticed before how wide the streets were in the old parts of Glasgow and how narrow they were in the new schemes, little grey ribbons which ran through the pale brown housing. The streets themselves seemed full of pale-faced children being rough with each other, far rougher than she had ever seen Italian children. Something else she noticed was how rarely, if ever, she had seen a solitary child. In Italy, it was not uncommon to see a child playing alone, but not here in this working city of contrasts. It seemed to her that if Glasgow children didn't run with the pack, they didn't run at all.

Less than twenty-four hours earlier she had walked with Rossi up the green-painted, canvas-awned gangplank of a floating discothèque and diner, where drink flowed easily and money changed hands rapidly. Now she sat next to Rossi in his car in a housing scheme, ten miles out of the city, where children, like the dogs, roamed in packs and the narrow streets were full of second-hand cars. She had the impression that money didn't change hands so rapidly here and when drink flowed, it flowed damagingly.

'I may make jokes about the low-life,' Rossi glanced round him, 'But this, I concede, is beyond a joke . And, I'll tell you something else, this is a lot better than it used to be.'

'Really?'

'Yes, really. This scheme's been re-vamped.'

'I wouldn't have believed it. And this is where Mickey Conner lives?'

'Well, it's where his mother lives, if you can call it living.' Rossi opened the car door. 'I'll be five minutes.'

'Perhaps, Dominic,' said Francesca, 'perhaps I could come with you, no?'

'If you like,' he said. 'Why not? You came to see Glasgow, well, this is her as much as the south side is.'

They left the car and walked up the path which led from the pavement to the street door. It ran between two patches of worn grass. The street door itself had an entry-phone system, common in Italy, but Francesca noticed that Rossi didn't attempt to use it, instead he simply pushed the door open.

'Never working,' he said and smiled. 'The kids bust the controlled entry systems as soon as the City installs them.'

She followed him into the close. It had been recently repainted – and recently re-graffitied. She read 'Fenian Drummie' but did not understand it.

The references to the Pope she did understand. She smelt a mustiness about the building, a strange smell which she had never encountered before.

'That's damp,' said Rossi, noticing her nose twitch and hearing her cough. 'The entire city is black with it. I can take you to homes where mushrooms grow out of the walls and that's the wall between the television and the gas fire.'

'Why don't the authorities do anything about it?' she asked as they began to climb the litter-strewn stairs. From inside one of the ground floor flats a huge dog began to bark.

'Oh, they do,' said Rossi. 'The Council visits, the man says "It's condensation", and tells people to open a window and keep it open.'

'That's unjust.' she said, stepping on a sweet wrapper which stuck to the sole of her shoe.

'It's criminal.' Rossi stopped at a door on the first floor landing. Francesca joined him. On the door was a name plate which read 'Conner', in gold, on a red tartan background. Rossi pressed the bell; nothing happened, so he rapped the letter-box, twice, in a manner which Francesca assumed had grown out of practice. It was loud, but not aggressive or threatening. Analysing it, she realised that the key to it was the space between the knocks; too rapid and it would have been aggressive, too great a time distance and it would have been ominous, threatening. She realised there was a skill in calling on people, and it began with how you announced your presence.

Mrs Conner proved to be a small, thin woman, who wore a cheap nylon cardigan around her shoulders. Her hair was long, unwashed, prematurely greying and straggling around her shoulders. She stood in the doorway, her arms folded; she eyed Rossi suspiciously and sniffed with contempt at Francesca.

'Mickey hasn't lived here for months, Mr . . . what did you say your name was?'

'Rossi,' said Rossi. 'Dominic Rossi.'

'Aye, Rossi,' she sniffed at Francesca again. A small girl appeared in the hallway behind Mrs Conner and the same musty smell began to emanate from the flat. 'Well, like I said, a few months, right enough. I couldn't blame him, they expected him to pay more than three hundred pounds for his poll tax, and that's to come out of his fifty-five pounds a week that he gets from humping boxes at the supermarket. That and driving the van. I don't know where he stays, I wouldn't tell you if I did, but he didn't tell me so I don't know and that's it.'

Francesca smiled at the little girl who stood in the hall. The little girl remained impassive, staring curiously at the tall elegant woman.

'Yes, I can understand that, Mrs Conner, but I'm here to help Mickey all I can.'

'Oh, what's he done now? There's more trouble, is there?'

'Maybe, perhaps not. It's information to help one of his mates really . . .'

'You're not making an awful lot of sense, Mr . . .'

'Rossi.'

'Mr Rossi . . . aye, odd name, foreign?'

'Italian.'

'Ha! Still you don't add up, first our Mickey's in trouble, then he isn't, then you want to help him. Then you want information; you going to tell me what's going on . . . and don't you go too far!' added Mrs Conner, as the small girl left the flat and went down the common stairs to the street door. 'See her, she's a mind of her own and no mistake. She's only eight and a right handful. I'm going to have more problems with her before the day's through, more problems than I've had with any of them. So, you're wanting to do our Mickey a favour, help him?'

'Aye,' said Rossi.

'Well, son, we all need all the help we can get, Mister . . .'

'Rossi.'

'Aye, Rossi, but where the hell are we going to get it?'

Rossi took a card from his breast pocket. 'That's my card,' he handed it to the woman. 'If you could give it to Mickey next time you see him, tell him it's urgent, he's just got to ring that number.'

'Can I tell him what it's about, no?'

'Tell him that it's about him and Gerard MacLawrie.'

'Young Gerard? I met him once. He's a nice lad.'

'Aye,' said Rossi sadly. 'Goodbye, Mrs Conner, thanks for your time.'

Rossi and Francesca turned away and the Conner's door slammed shut behind them. They walked down the stairs, narrow concrete stairs, plastered walls, red up to chest height, then cream. Most of the graffiti was on the cream paint.

'See what I mean about victims,' said Rossi. 'That stuff about poll tax, that's what it means in reality. People, young vulnerable people, being forced from their homes, not telling their parents where they are . . .'

'I know that,' she said softly, knowledgeably.

Rossi glanced back at her, surprised, pleased, impressed. 'I didn't know that you were a student of politics?'

'Student, well, that's a bit generous,' she replied, 'but I'd like to think that I keep myself informed. Once, years ago, I was very keen.'

'Oh.' They turned the stair. At the foot of the stair-case, at the entrance to the close, Mrs Conner's little girl stood, looking up at them.

'Yes,' Francesca continued, 'I held strong views. I

don't now . . . ' she broke off as she noticed Mrs Conner's girl.

They approached her. Francesca crouched before the girl and caressed her hair. Rossi sank back against the wall. Francesca, he thought, knew exactly what she was doing.

'I visit him,' said the girl.

'Who?' asked Francesca, gently.

'Mickey. I visit him. Tony, my other big brother, he takes me.'

Where does Mickey live?' asked Francesca. 'We're his friends and it's important for us to talk to him.'

'On the site.' said the girl.

'The site?'

'Aye, the caravan site.'

Francesca turned and glanced at Rossi, who whispered, 'which one?'

'Which one?' said Francesca. 'Which caravan site?'

The girl shrugged her shoulders. Francesca turned to Rossi.

'How does she get there?' prompted Rossi.

'How do you get there?'

'By train, we get the train into the town and then we get the underground. I count the stops and when I count eight, we get off.'

'What's the place like where you get off the tube, hen?' said Rossi, over Francesca's shoulder.

Privately, Francesca thought that Scottish girls

should not grow up in the habit of being addressed as 'hen', but there was no doubt that Rossi had managed to reach her, because the girl beamed at him, and said, 'It's a bus station, a new bus station, and shops.'

Rossi smiled. 'The site, hen, what's the caravan like?'

'Sort of long and square.'

'What colour is it?'

'Green. Green and cream. A bit like the close.' She nodded to the walls. 'Only green, not red.'

'Green on the bottom, white on top?' said Rossi, and the girl nodded.

'Where's the van in the camp? At the entrance, next to the road?'

The girl shook her head. 'Past the big black dog.' she said.

'You're a wee pal, hen,' said Rossi and gave her a fifty-pence piece.

Rossi and Francesca walked out of the close and back towards Rossi's car. She was surprised it hadn't been vandalised and it showed.

'They just don't.' he said as he opened the passenger door for her. 'They just don't get damaged in the schemes. I don't know why it should be, but they don't. If my car's going to get vandalised, it will be in the town, or up the west end or the south side. I can't tell you the number of times I've left my motor parked in the schemes when I've had to travel out to take a witness's statement and expected to come back to a body shell or a burnt out wreck. But it's just never happened.'

'It's strange,' she said, sliding onto the seat. 'I think in Italy it would not be so.'

They didn't speak again until Rossi had joined the M8 and they were cruising towards the city. Francesca broke the silence, asking him if he knew where the caravan site was.

'It'll be in Govan.' he said. 'If they get the train into the town, they'll get off at Queen Street; the tube's a simple circle line, eight stops on the tube from Queen St is either Ibrox or Govan. She described a new bus station and shops; that's Govan. So I'll pay a call on young Mickey Conner tomorrow. Though, this time, I'll go alone, if you don't mind.'

'As you wish,' she said.

They drove on. There was a short silence, broken by Rossi:

'Do you mind if I ask you something?'

She anticipated the question. 'Sergio's father is someone I met a long time ago. It's all in the past. Does that answer your question?'

Rossi nodded. 'Partly; can I ask why you didn't marry?'

'Well,' she said defensively, 'why didn't you?'

'My mother never thought anyone was up to the job.'

'Neither did mine,' she said, smiling. 'The Arcalli's are a proud family.'

There was another silence.

'What do you want to do for the rest of the night?' he asked, 'not to mention the rest of my life?'

Francesca smiled and laid a slender hand on his thigh. 'Just take me home, Dominic. I don't want to go anywhere else tonight.'

Chapter 6

THE DAY BEGAN dull and overcast but remained dry. That morning, Rossi and Francesca seemed to have awakened at precisely the same moment. He had often noticed it, that when a relationship is fresh, he and his lady often awoke at the same moment, often knowing the other was also awake and they just began to talk. It was only when the relationship began to mature that one could wake up alone, slip out from the sheets, slip back again without waking the other. It was when his relationships began to reach that stage that Dominic Rossi began to hunt new thighs.

He didn't think he would do that with Francesca. For the first time in his life, he felt he had found someone with whom he wanted not just to spend the rest of his life but, more than that, someone to whom he wanted to devote the rest of his life.

That morning, about an hour after they had woken up, Rossi eased himself out of the bed. He went downstairs and made coffee; one cup he left in the kitchen, the other he took back upstairs and placed beside Francesca who lay with her head on one side, wearing an expression of deep contentment and peace.

'I have to go out,' he said softly. 'I'll be back in the late afternoon.'

She nodded and smiled at him.

'Don't do anything too strenuous today,' he added, padding out of the bedroom, 'we're going out this evening.'

'I'll remember that,' she said lazily.

Rossi drove to Govan. He parked his car and asked a police officer where he might find a caravan site near to the bus station. The officer eyed him quizzically and then pointed him towards the river.

Rossi found the site without difficulty. Like most caravan sites, it occupied an area of wasteground between blocks of tenements. Clearly it had once been an area of tenements itself because the small road which ran through the centre of the site, between caravans, lorries and fairground equipment, was cobbled.

Rossi walked onto the site, aware of looks from men working on equipment, from women in caravans who sat at the windows and drew back their lace curtains as he passed, observing him.

A black labrador ambled into the cobbled roadway, turned and sank, curling up. It was an old dog, white around the snout, overweight. Once it would have bounded snarling up to the stranger on the territory, now it just eyed Rossi with lazy disinterest. But it meant he was on the right track. Beyond the black

131

dog, Rossi saw to his left a long square caravan, lilac below cream. It was the sort of lilac that a small girl would call green.

He walked towards it, anxious now to reach it because by knocking on the door he gave a legitimate reason for being on the site; he was a visitor, calling on someone. As soon as he knocked on the door people would be less suspicious; some might continue to watch him, others, satisfied, would go about their business.

By knocking on the door, he would show that he wasn't a smug 'townie', prowling around the site, amusing himself by looking at the way 'tinks' live; the sort of action that would invite a response from the aforementioned 'tinks' little short of murder.

Rossi marched boldly up to the door and rapped on it. Out of the corner of his eye, he saw a man turn away and carry on filling a bucket from a standpipe.

There was no answer. He stepped to one side and, turned to peer through the window, but it was too high. He looked around; a discarded milk crate would do nicely. He dragged the crate up to the caravan and stood on it and peered through the window. A narrow table, some beer cans, a small calor gas stove. . . The crate jerked, he fell backwards, recovered, turned and faced three men. Young. Hard. Menacing. Angry.

'What do you want, pal?' said one, the middle one,

ready to throw a punch at any second.

Rossi kept calm outwardly, but his legs were jelly. He knew that these guys could put the boot in and nobody would see anything. They knew that themselves. 'I'm looking for Mickey Conner,' he said.

'Never heard of him. Beat it – pal.'

'Look, relax will you. I've got nothing to do with the council and I'm not interested in registering you for the poll tax.' He paused. 'Any of you guys got a cigarette?'

The three men looked at him.

'You're not the law or the council?' said one.

'No.' Rossi shook his head.

'You're a pal of Mickey's?'

'Sort of.'

'I think we'll go inside,' said the first. 'Too many eary-wigs around here.'

The caravan was cramped. Rossi and the three youths sat round the table. A can of beer and a fag were pushed into Rossi's hands. 'You're OK,' said the first man and told Rossi what he knew about Mickey Conner. When he had finished speaking, Rossi said:

'What Chinese job?'

'Don't know,' said the first man. 'He just said that he'd be able to move out of here; you know, back home; he wouldn't be a poll tax embarrassment any more, not once he'd done this Chinese job. Not once he'd got the money. But he wouldn't say any more about it – at least, no' to me.'

The other two shook their heads, confirming what the young man said.

'And you're sure he never said which job he was doing for these Chinese guys?'

'Like we said.'

'When was the last time you saw him?'

'Sunday night,' said the second man, a thin youth, with a drawn face. 'Was that the night that his pal got run over?'

Rossi nodded. 'Sunday; two days ago now.'

'Wouldn't have been Mickey,' said the third youth. 'Really. Mickey's a bit bent, but he wouldn't do a thing like that. He's just not the type.'

Rossi persisted. 'Did he say anything at all that you can remember – on Sunday night, I mean?'

'The only thing I can remember is Mickey being in one hell of a hurry to get to a phone,' said the third youth. 'He went on about getting in touch with the guy who could fix it for him.'

'Fix what?'

'It,' said the youth. 'Whatever "it" was.'

Rossi took a card from his breast pocket and laid it on the table. 'That's me.'

'Notary public.' The first youth read it, 'what's that?'

'Solicitor.' Rossi stood. 'If you see Mickey, ask him

to get in touch as soon as he likes. It's in his interest to do so.'

*   *   *

Francesca lay in Rossi's bed. She listened to him dress, heard him leave the house, the car door opening and then slamming shut. She listened as the car engine roared into life and the wheels crunched over the gravel. Then all was silent save the distant hum of traffic from the motorway. She lay in bed until 10.30 and then slid smoothly from the sheets, bathed and dressed in casual clothes. She went downstairs and made herself a mug of coffee and carried it through to the living-room. In the kitchen, the sight of the wall-mounted telephone had planted an idea in her mind. The idea gestated during the walk from the kitchen to the living-room and by the time she reached the living-room, it was fully formed. She placed the mug of coffee on a table and picked up the phone.

She dialled slowly and methodically. She held the receiver to her ear and waited; she heard a series of clicks penetrate a silence and then, eventually, a ringing tone filled her ears.

'It's Francesca,' she said when the phone was answered. 'No, I cannot tell you where I am, Mother. No, but I am well . . . yes, I'd like to talk to Sergio . . . hello, hello Sergio . . . it's Mama . . . hello . . . darling . . . I had to phone you to wish you happy birthday.

Yes, very happy birthday . . . you be good, darling. I'll see you soon. . . . Do what Grandmama and Vincenzo ask. I have to go now. Goodbye. . .. Goodbye.'

She replaced the receiver but kept her hand on it. She paused and then lifted it and dialled another number, equally slowly, equally methodically. Again, she waited as the clicks penetrated the silence. She heard a ringing tone, it rang for a full minute before it was answered.

'Guilo,' she said. 'It's me, Francesca, . . . in Glasgow, yes Scotland . . . I'm fine . . . no problems . . . I am safe here . . . anything at your end? . . . no, I can't tell you exactly where I am but I can give you this number to reach me if there is an emergency . . . have you a pen? . . . good, it is one, eight, three, zero, three, eight, nine, four, nine. I have to go, don't call me unless you have to . . . take care.'

In his room, in Rome, Guilo scribbled down the numbers that Francesca had read out to him. He then subtracted seven from each number and wrote down four, one, six, three, six, one, two, seven, two. He folded the paper and placed it inside a book.

In a basement, also in Rome, not two kilometres from where Guilio sat in his dingy room, hiding from whoever was systematically killing his comrades, another man also wrote down the numbers that Francesca Arcalli dictated. He sat at a desk, wearing headphones. He dialled the number that had been dictated and when the long, monotonous 'number unobtainable' tone filled his ears, he replaced the receiver. He looked at the numbers as he had written them. So they used a code. Codes can be cracked, often very easily, especially numerical codes. The man rubbed his hand through his hair, grateful that here in the basement he did not have to wear the wig.

*　　*　　*

'Do you always get doors slammed in your face?' Rossi approached Cowan as the lady shut the door on her prospective Labour party representative. On the road, a van drove slowly by, loudspeakers attached to the roof, the man on the passenger seat spoke into the microphone urging voters to 'Vote for Gerry Cowan. Vote Labour'.

Cowan shrugged. 'Win some, lose some, I guess,' he said, turning to Rossi. He wore a huge red rosette on his left shoulder. 'Have you come to lend your support to the campaign vehicle?'

'Afraid not,' said Rossi, 'though, of course, I wish you every success. I'd like a couple of minutes of your time, please. I need to pick your brains about matters Chinese.'

'How can I help?'

'Well, the Chinese community is a pretty closed one, is it not. Very closeknit?'

137

Cowan nodded. 'Very much so.'

'So, what kind of job would a couple of young Glasgow Tearaways be doing for them that produced eighteen thousand pounds? I mean, that's a lot of pennies.'

'Certainly is. Two of them you say?'

'Yeah,' said Rossi. 'Apparently they panicked when they got caught by the boys in blue and started blaming each other. My guess is that they were both in on it. Whatever "it" was.'

'Eighteen thousand.' Cowan spoke softly. 'Do either of them have form for robbery?'

'I don't know about one, Mickey Conner, but I'm reliably informed that his whole family is a bad lot, so he's probably got form for everything under the sun. Gerard MacLawrie's family have a long tradition of honourable theft.'

'What's honourable theft?' Cowan grinned.

'Well, a big house in the West End is a legitimate target for burglary but not a pensioner's flat in an east-end scheme. That's what I mean. Why do you ask?'

'Well, it occurs to me that there's a possibility; it's remote but it's a stone worth turning over. You know that Chinese are keen gamblers; well, they've got these gambling dens of their own, mobile ones, by which I mean that they move them around from place to place. Strictly illegal, you see.'

'And?' Rossi pressed Cowan.

'Well, there's thousands of pounds changing hands and I've heard whispers that these dens have been turned over a few times. It never gets reported to the police, of course, because it's dirty money. So perhaps that's what they did.'

'I see,' Rossi pondered. 'It's food for thought, right enough. So somebody from the Chinese community, a hit man, catches up with Gerard MacLawrie, fills him in, in the time honoured manner and Mickey, not surprisingly, does a runner. Yeah, that fits together nicely, thanks.'

'No problem.' Cowan nodded. 'Anyway, if you'll excuse me, I have doors on which to knock.'

Rossi returned to the caravan site. Again he walked down the cobbled street, again he walked past the old black dog, aware of curtains moving as he went by. He went straight to the lilac and cream caravan and knocked on the door.

No answer.

He tried the door. It was open.

He paused. It was a risk.

Inside the caravan, he rummaged quickly behind cushions, under mattresses. Stuffed behind a chair cushion he found a folded sheet of paper. It seemed to be a rough hand sketch of a building, doors, stairs and exits being clearly marked. Rossi grinned. 'Gerry Cowan, you're a genius.' he said, as he left the caravan, closing the door behind him.

He walked hurriedly out of the caravan site, aware once again of people watching him. He was not, though, aware of one man who sat in a car, parked on the other side of the road outside the site. That man was Detective Inspector Ballantyne, who the previous week had been boxed into a corner by the mental agility of Eleanor Goodchild. He watched Rossi, tapping his fingers thoughtfully on his steering wheel as he did so.

*   *   *

She had a beautiful back. Rossi reflected that backs were as erotic and sensual and sexual as any other part of the female anatomy and Francesca Arcalli had, in Rossi's not inconsiderable experience, a particularly beautiful back; slender, with sharply delineated shoulder blades. Earlier that evening, he had tapped reverently on the bathroom door, enquiring if she would like him to scrub her back. She had replied with a pleasant laugh that she could manage herself. 'There will be other baths,' he had said to himself as he walked away. A little later, by means of compensation, she had asked him to zip her up. He had run the zip up the back of her dress easily and smoothly.

Rossi left the bedroom and walked downstairs, his tie hanging untied around his neck, fixing his cufflinks as he skipped lightly down the stairs. He walked into the living-room and stood in front of the mirror, turning his attention to his tie.

The phone rang.

He turned from the mirror, crossed the floor and picked up the receiver.

'Hello,' he said absent-mindedly, automatically, 'six, three, six, one, two, seven two. . .' The sound on the line had a distant, hollow and echoing quality. A voice, a foreign accent, said in English, 'Pardon.'

Rossi said, 'What? This is six three six, one two seven two. What number are you calling? . . . Dominic Rossi speak . . .'

The caller hung up.

Rossi frowned, shrugged, replaced the receiver and returned to the mirror and tied his tie. He fumbled, he made a mess of it at the first attempt, tore the tie open and re-tied it, but he was on edge, he had to force himself to concentrate. The phone call was curious, it puzzled him. No, it didn't; it didn't puzzle him at all.

It upset him. For some reason he could not put his finger on, he was upset by the call. It was an international call, that was certain. It had that unmistakeable sense of speaking to someone across a large empty room. He presumed it had come from Italy. He didn't at all mind Francesca making or receiving calls, but there was something sinister about that call; something probing.

He sat on a chair pondering the call and stood as

Francesca entered the room, elegant in a dark dress, matching handbag and shoes.

'Do I look all right?' she turned on her heels, smiling, anticipating the answer.

'Oh, I think you'll take the place by storm. Shall we go?'

Francesca walked towards the door. Rossi followed, glanced again at the phone, 'Were you expecting a call?' he asked suddenly, speaking before thinking.

'No, why?' Francesca stopped and turned.

'Somebody rang, a few minutes ago, didn't say anything expect "pardon" in a foreign accent, just a bit slurred perhaps, but I couldn't tell, the line wasn't good. It sounded like an international call.'

'It means nothing to me,' she said casually and continued to walk out of the room.

Rossi followed her, unconvinced. He was a lawyer, he was therefore a good actor, and like any good actor he could detect theatricals in others. Francesca's casual shrugging off of the incident was a little too studied. It was the action of somebody with something to hide.

*   *   *

Guilo replaced the phone. He sank drunkenly onto the bed and reached for the bottle. The glass he had used was now on its side on the floor.

He no longer cared. He drank straight from the bottle.

His room was small. Dingy. The walls were closing in.

Suddenly, he heard loud voices in the corridor. He shot upright and then relaxed as the voices receded.

He drank deeply from the bottle. The room began to swim. Now there was only him, and Francesca, and Pietro. Pietro was killing them. He wanted to talk to Francesca. Alone in the room, just him and the bottles of brandy, day in day out, he wanted to talk to Francesca. He had to talk to somebody and Francesca was the only person he could talk to.

He had resisted calling her, resisted as long as he was able but the deprivation of human company, his racing imagination had overcome his will to resist. So he had dialled the number which she had given him. He just needed to hear her voice, to be reassured that he wasn't alone in the world.

A man had answered.

Guilo had mumbled something out of sheer sinking disappointment and the man had continued to talk, sounding calm, assured, no one stalking him, no bullet in the head for him any second, any minute. Francesca had done well for herself, got well away.

She had deserted him.

The thought had come to Guilo in an instant. It came suddenly and lodged permanently. He was alone. The number she had given was probably false. She could be traced to that number, so it had to be false. Francesca Arcalli, he remembered, always had an eye for the main chance, always placed herself before the others, she was a survivor.

Even when the bomb had gone off, she had contrived to be at a party the previous night, establishing an alibi.

Certainly, the bomb could not have been planted without the information she provided, but when it did go off, with all the devastation that had been planned, the finger of suspicion was never once pointed at her.

Now she had fled again, covering her tracks, living somewhere in the UK but, wherever it was, it would not be at the house of the man called Rossi.

Bitterly, Guilo gulped the brandy, drinking himself into unconsciousness.

*   *   *

Carlo tapped the pencil on his desk and studied the information he had scribbled on his note pad, a number 636 1272 and a name 'Rossi'.

He quickly triplicated the information by hand and placed the two copies in separate locations. One in a file, one in a drawer. That done, he relaxed; he could not afford to lose the information. So he had a telephone number. It could be a Glasgow telephone number; earlier she had said she was in Glasgow. It might have been a code she was using just as she had used a code to relay the phone number. Glasgow might mean Bristol, Birmingham, anywhere. But it might also mean Glasgow.

Toying idly with possibilities, he consulted a previous page of his note pad and wrote down the telephone number given earlier by Francesca. Scribbling rapidly, he found that if the figure seven was subtracted from that number, the result was the number given out by the man called Rossi.

Carlo grinned. Francesca Arcalli was at that number. And if that number was in Glasgow, then she could be traced.

He leaned forward and picked up the phone on his desk. He dialled a two-figure internal number . . . he paused and then spoke 'Hello, switchboard? Yes, can you put me through to the Central Post Office . . . Yes, here in Rome . . .' Carlo waited. The line clicked and then rang. 'Hello, Post Office? *Carabinieri* here . . . yes, do you have a current edition of the Glasgow telephone directory . . . you should have . . . good . . . I'd like some information . . . well it's public information but you can phone me back if you insist . . .. ask for extension 2117 . . .. The name of the subscriber is ROSSI . . . the number is six-three-six, one-two-seven-two . . . I'd like the address of that number . . . I know that Rossi is a common Italian name, but how many Rossis do you think there are in Glasgow? Thank you. I'll await your call.'

He had to wait for ninety seconds. His phone rang, he said, 'Two-one-one-seven, . . . thank you, put him on . . . hello . . . oh, I see, no listing at all . . . and that is the current telephone directory . . . thank you.'

Carlo replaced the receiver but kept his hand on it. He picked it up and dialled another two-figure internal number. It rang out. He waited patiently. It was answered. 'Hello . . . yes, hello, this is two-one-one-seven . . . Interpol request . . . from *Carabinieri*, Rome to Anti-Terrorist Squad, New Scotland yard, London . . . name Rossi . . . telephone number six-three-six one-two-seven-two . . . believed to be a Glasgow number . . . address of that telephone number, please. Thank you.' He replaced the receiver and glanced at his watch. 8.30 p.m. Quite enough work for one day.

He stood and reached for his jacket. He fancied a beer, a couple of glasses before returning to his flat. It was often the way of it, he reflected, as he left the building, stepping into the street and becoming one of the crowd. You can bang your head against a brick wall for days on end and get nowhere and then the case cracks wide open in a matter of seconds, as in this case. Even if that phone number wasn't a Glasgow number, he thought, how long could it take the computerised British Telecom to identify the location of any given name and number? One hour, two?

Yes, he felt that this evening he could indulge in a beer or two.

*   *   *

'Dominic told me that you were the most beautiful woman he had ever met.' Sinclair Murray bowed slightly as he kissed Francesca's hand. 'I'm pleased that he has finally told the truth, the whole truth and nothing but the truth! The truth, I believe should always be told without economy and without embellishment.'

Francesca laughed softly; Rossi raised his eyes to the ceiling. They stood in the restaurant foyer, deeply carpeted, softly illuminated.

'Shall we dine?' Sinclair Murray said to Francesca, offering his arm with a grace and social polish which forced even Rossi, with his hard-bitten cynicism, to be impressed, albeit grudgingly.

Francesca accepted Sinclair Murray's arm and, with Rossi following, they walked into the dining-room. They ate while making gentle conversation. A female singer stood on a dais wearing an evening gown. She sang soft, romantic melodies to the accompaniment of a grand piano played with an acutely sensitive touch by a handsome youth in a dinner jacket.

'The decoration in here evokes Rennie Mackintosh,' said Rossi, as the conversation entered a lull.

'Who?' asked Francesca.

'Rennie Mackintosh,' repeated Rossi, 'celebrated Glasgow architect and designer; he designed powerfully angled buildings, and chairs just like these ones with tall thin backs.

'I see,' said Francesca. 'There are buildings of his in Glasgow.'

'Most certainly.' said Rossi. 'The Glasgow School of Art is possibly the most famous, a church in Maryhill is also oft photographed.'

'I'd like to see his work,' said Francesca, manipulating her knife and fork with cultivated delicacy. 'I'm an interior designer myself.'

'We'll make it the theme of the second tour of the city,' said Rossi. He turned to Sinclair Murray and explained, 'The first tour was Glasgow, her museums and art treasures.'

'And a bit of low-life,' Francesca added.

'And a bit of low-life,' Rossi conceded. 'So trip two will be Glasgow, her architecture.'

'There's plenty to see there,' said Sinclair Murray. 'You know, I feel bound to say that your English is very good.'

'I have no excuse for it not being,' Francesca replied. 'I spent three years at the LSE.'

'Now, I didn't know that they taught interior design there.'

Francesca laughed. 'It sounds indulgent, but I got

bored with politics and economics. Besides, interior design pays better.'

'That's what it's all about,' said Rossi, a gentle note of disapproval in his voice.

'What did your family think of that?' Sinclair Murray spoke quickly before Francesca could rise to Rossi's tone.

'I didn't ask their opinion,' she said finally, flatly. 'Tell me, Mr Sinclair Murray, do you think Dominic will make a good advocate?' Francesca finished her meal.

'I'm not sure he's really decided, have you Dominic?'

'Well, the jury's expected back any time now, can't put the decision off for ever.'

'Dominic is only good for that modern jumping up and down dancing,' Sinclair Murray spoke to Francesca, 'but this,' he nodded towards the dance floor, 'this is my forte. Shall we?'

'I'd love to.' Francesca slung her handbag onto the rear of the chair and stood.

'Private education.' Sinclair Murray smiled at Rossi as he stood. 'Benefits of same.'

As Francesca and Sinclair Murray walked onto the dance floor, the singer and the pianist stopped playing and acknowledged the applause. Pre-recorded music began to play. Sinclair Murray and Francesca turned and held each other. The singer left the dais and walked across the floor and into the dining area. She weaved between the tables and, passing the table at which Rossi sat, quite by accident dislodged Francesca's bag. It fell to the floor and a few items spilled out, her passport amongst them.

Idly, Rossi leant over and picked it up, opening it as he did so. His expectant grin was rapidly replaced by a frown as he read the details. Stunned, openmouthed, he looked up and stared at Francesca, dancing gracefully with Sinclair Murray.

They taxied to Rossi's house. Sinclair Murray and Francesca played table tennis, very badly, thought Rossi, but with great enjoyment. Rossi sat in the corner of the room and he found himself looking at Francesca with growing suspicion. The details of the passport had filled him with a sudden yet immense disappointment which, as the evening wore on, was replaced by a suspicion, a suspicion of the woman's true identity and, out of that, grew a suspicion of the woman's motives.

Whenever she glanced at him he would smile, but when her back was turned his expression returned to one of concern and suspicion. Later still, when Sinclair Murray had left to return home, Rossi retired quickly and pretended to be asleep as Francesca glided into the room on tip-toe. He lay facing outwards and, as he felt Francesca slide under the duvet as gently as she could and nestle into the mattress, he opened his eyes.

*   *   *

There was a note lying in his in-tray when he arrived at his desk the following morning. His head was heavy, his speech still slurred. The two or three beers he had promised himself had, in the course of the evening, stretched to double figures and had gone on to involve wine. At least so far as he recalled, he had drunk some wine. He sat heavily at his desk and reached for the envelope which lay in his in-tray and tore it open. It contained a telex message from Interpol. 'With reference to the *Carabinieri*'s request' . . . and provided an address in Glasgow. Carlo studied the address. It seemed a strange name to his eyes. It was a place called Pollokshaws.

He grinned.

'Cracking open,' he said to himself. 'After ten years, it's cracking wide open.' He reached forward and picked up his phone and dialled, 'Flights to Scotland, details of,' he said, when his call was answered. 'Today please, if I could be in Glasgow by this evening . . . . Yes, a seat on the next available flight. . . . This is two one one seven. *Grazie*.'

*   *   *

Rossi and Flanagan stepped out of the Chinese restaurant onto Great Western Road. The tall, thin spire of the Episcopalian church stood to their right, a shored-up tenement opposite. Small shops lined the pavement: Indian grocers', Asian garment shops, small newsagents, a motor-cycle retailer. There were tenements above the shops, vast six- or seven-roomed flats, with the more desirable property lining the gardens which led away from the road at right angles. It was a dry day; fresh wind with a low sky. Rossi and Flanagan fell into step with each other. On their right, four lanes of traffic growled relentlessly, composed mainly, it seemed to Rossi, of black taxis and orange buses.

'Nice contact there,' said Flanagan. 'I mean never look a freebie in the face.'

'Handy,' Rossi agreed, but his mind was elsewhere. 'We're doing some work for them. It ought to be good for us, it's a foothold in the Chinese community, if we can get recommended by word of mouth . . .'

'Snowball effect.' Flanagan began to eat his fortune cookie.

'That's it,' Rossi did the same. 'Word of mouth is always the strongest recommendation. One satisfied customer leads to another.' He read the motto from his cookie, ' "The face of authority is never marked" – whatever that means.'

'I guess it means you don't claw your way to the top

without accumulating a few battle scars on the way. Angelic faces may be appealing but their owners haven't been through the mill.'

'You should have been a philosopher.' Rossi grinned. 'So, what does yours say?'

'Mine,' said Flanagan, unfolding the paper. 'Oh, now, hear this as thought for the day – "A man is accountable to his parents but responsible for his friends".'

'Very Chinese,' said Rossi. 'The authority of the parent is deeply rooted in Oriental culture, so I believe. Much more so than in the West.'

'So I believe. Well, we got the meal on the house, but little else. Now where do we go?'

'Find a pub somewhere and plan our next move. You know, I half-thought that they might talk to me, what with the money we've already saved them. Did I tell you they were all for buying this building cash in hand and virtually sight unseen?'

'No.'

'Yes, and this wide boy would have sold it to them as well. He knew about the mine workings underneath and wanted out fast.'

'Can't blame him.'

'Yes, but they're our clients. We got a survey for a couple of hundred quid and saved them a couple of hundred thousand, so I guess the free meal was a bit cheap at the price.'

'No wonder we got service with a smile.'

'I was hoping that their gratitude would extend to providing a little information about Chinatown on Clyde. I suppose I was a bit naïve.'

Flanagan nodded, 'I think you were, oh eminent Rossi! I think we'll have to wait until Mickey Conner turns up; meanwhile we can still ferret around after the truth.'

'Oh yeah, the truth,' said Rossi sourly.

*   *   *

He was disorientated. Suddenly, after all the rush, he was exhausted. He picked his bag up from the carousel and walked to the bar, bought a coffee, sat and sipped it, trying to collect his thoughts. He had been in Rome at 9.30 that morning when the phone call came through: Could he be at the airport in an hour? Damn right he could, with the help of a police vehicle, a flashing light and a siren which stopped at his apartment *en route* so that he could throw a few things including a 9mm automatic into an overnight bag. He was waived through customs by courtesy of diplomatic privilege and arrived in London at 1300 hours. He had transferred to the Glasgow shuttle and now sat in the lounge of Glasgow Airport, trying to let the events of the day catch him up. He sat for an hour, had three coffees. This was only his second trip to the UK and his first to Scotland. When he had at last collected his thoughts and when he felt a little more accustomed to his surroundings, he walked from the lounge. He passed the row of seats which looked out onto the apron where school boys with short-wave receivers sat, listening to the transmissions between the pilots and the control tower. He went down the escalator to the foyer and hired a car from Avis.

'Oh,' he said, 'I wish for to buy a map of the roads of Glasgow; where is there a shop for this?'

'Any newsagents, sir,' smiled the smartly dressed girl.

'Newsagent, what is?'

'A shop which sells newspapers, sir. Any one will stock a street directory.'

'*Grazie*,' said Carlo, more comfortable in his wig in the cooler climate of Scotland.

*   *   *

All day, Rossi could not get rid of an intense sense of irritation. That morning, after he had hurriedly left the house before Francesca awoke, he had attempted to fill his head with work but found his pen moving faster and his signature less legible than usual. He had smiled at Shona and overheard her advising Paul that, whatever he did, he had better not go into 'Mr Rossi's' office this morning. Later he had crossed swords with Eleanor Goodchild. The matter was personal and, on the scale of things, utterly trifling but an onlooker would have been forgiven for thinking that the life of one or the other had depended on the outcome. Then there had been the lunch with Flanagan. Though it hadn't been wholly successful because they had failed to get any information about the Chinese community, Flanagan's company had helped him calm down. Despite his red-blooded lust for female flesh, in times of personal crisis, it was the company of male friends that he sought. After lunch, they had had a beer and then gone their separate ways; Flanagan back to his 'people's lawyer surgery' in Drumchapel and Rossi, alone again, walked from Woodlands into the city, still fuming about the details in Francesca's passport, or, at least, the passport which had fallen out of Francesca's bag.

Who on earth was she?

He had stormed back into his office, kicked the door open and then kicked it shut behind him, aware of – but utterly unconcerned about – the looks thrown at him by Shona and Paul. When he had emerged three hours later, he had found the reception area empty, Shona and Paul having diplomatically slipped away home on the stroke of five.

Rossi returned home, forcing an emotional detachment upon himself as a not wholly healthy means of controlling his anger. He parked the car in front of his house, noticing, but not concerned about, the man sitting in a parked car opposite his house. He went inside and walked to the back of the house, to the kitchen, still wearing his overcoat, still carrying his briefcase.

Francesca was in the kitchen. She leant over the hob, tasting the sauce for the spaghetti as he opened the door. Had he been in a less troubled frame of mind, he would have savoured the rich variety of scents and smells which assailed his nostrils. In the event, the only emotion he could muster was dry hostility.

'National stereotype day, is it?' he said coldly, sarcastically. Francesca looked round, sensing his tone.

'The sauce will be another half hour. Is something perhaps wrong, Dominic? Was the day bad?'

'Let's you and I make a deal, OK?' He placed his briefcase down by the wall just beneath the telephone. 'I'll get into the right mood over the spaghetti and you can tell me the story of your life.'

'Dominic, I've told you.' Francesca was puzzled. 'Perhaps you have forgotten the day it rained in Sorrento.'

'Well, that's just it,' said Rossi. 'That's the issue. I haven't forgotten the day it rained in Sorrento, nor have I forgotten anything that was said that day.'

'So, where is the problem?'

'We'll talk over dinner.' he said. 'I'll open some wine.'

Over dinner, Francesca broke the silence, 'Where

do you want me to start?'

'You decide.' said Rossi. He sipped his wine, but toyed with the meal.

Francesca paused. 'I was born on June 16, in 1957.'

'Oh,' said Rossi, 'frankly you couldn't have chosen a better place to start – or a worse place – depending on your point of view.'

'What do you mean?'

Rossi rose from the table and left the kitchen. He returned a few moments later holding Francesca's passport. He dropped it in front of her.

'It fell out of your bag last night in the restaurant, just in case you were about to get on your high horse about me going into your bags or through your personal possessions . . .'

'Dominic . . . I . . .'

'I just wondered, you see. I wondered what your passport photograph was like because they're always awful. Everybody knows that.' He found his voice rising. 'But even allowing for that, that photograph isn't you. Hell, I mean the photograph is you, but the name is not yours, the address is different, the date of birth is months out.' He paused, collected himself as Francesca stared, open-mouthed at the passport. 'It's a false passport, Francesca. If that is your name. You're in my house, you share my bed . . . I'd be obliged in the name of honesty, decency and sheer honest-to-God good manners, if you would kindly tell me what's going on.'

'None of your business,' she said, defensively, after a long silence.

'What do you mean, none of my business?' Rossi shouted, unable to control his temper. 'I've practically asked you to marry me.'

The phone rang.

Rossi glared at it. Then he stormed across the floor and snatched it from the wall. 'Yes!' he said and then sank against the wall as he listened. He replaced the receiver and walked out of the kitchen. He returned, his raincoat hanging round his shoulders. He looked at Francesca.

'They've found Mickey's body – you know, Gerard MacLawrie's pal. I have to go out. . . . It'll give you time to think up some answers and, by that, I don't mean that you have time to think up some fanciful story, some fabrication. I mean, you've got an hour or two to work out the best way of telling the truth.'

*   *   *

Carlo was many things. He was an assassin, he was a lover of opera, but first and foremost, he was a cop. As a cop, he was a trained observer. He sat in the hired car opposite the house in Pollokshaws in the dull and overcast rainy city of Glasgow and found it little wonder that Alban, and the dreaded Antonine wall, further north even than the loathed Hadrian's wall, was the most hated posting for the Legionnaires of ancient Rome. How they must have dreamed and longed for the blue skies of home when mounting their lonely guard in this island of dark cloud and rain and swirling mist.

The door of the house opened. Carlo sank back in the seat. The man who had arrived forty minutes earlier left again hurriedly, walking quickly to his car and driving rapidly away.

Carlo the cop, Carlo the trained observer, could tell the actions of a man who was leaving home on a pressing errand and who would not be back for some time; sufficient time for him to do what he had come to do and then catch the midnight train to London, the first stage of the journey home.

He glanced at himself in the rear-view mirror. The wig sat well on his head. He checked the automatic; full magazine, safety catch off. He left the car and walked towards the large, eerie-looking house.

*   *   *

Rossi drove to the east end, close to the old building that was Templeton's Carpet Factory which, by design, echoed the Doge's Palace in Rome. He drove to where the Clyde slid softly and silently through the lush expanse of Glasgow Green.

He walked up to where Flanagan stood, watching a police operation. Orange ribbon cordoned off a section of river bank, a body was being brought from the shallows. Flanagan turned as Rossi approached.

'Hi,' he said.

'Hi,' Rossi nodded. 'Thanks for giving me a bell. Sure it's Mickey?'

'Yeah,' said Flanagan sourly. 'It's him, all right.'

'Did he drown?'

'Makes a variation on the old theme of falling or being pushed. Cop I spoke to says that he's got a ligature round his neck, a piece of wire.' Flanagan leaned forward, looking behind Rossi. 'Top boy in blue, ahoy.' he said. 'Don't look now, but here comes your friend and mine.'

'Ballantyne?' asked Rossi.

'The one and the same.'

'Funny how he keeps popping up,' said Rossi.

Ballantyne came close to where Rossi and Flanagan stood, looked beyond them for a moment as the body was laid on the grass, and then turned to them.

'I think it's time we had a full and frank discussion, gentlemen,' he said. 'I think that you know more than you're letting on. I think it's odd you keep turning up in all the wrong places.'

'Funny you should say that,' said Rossi.

'Don't know what you mean, Inspector,' said Flanagan. 'We know nothing. Nothing at all.'

*   *   *

Rossi drove home. His house was in darkness. He left his car and walked towards the house and then stopped in his tracks.

The front door of his house lay open.

Even if she had left, she would have closed the door. His heart thumped, his body tensed, yet at the same time his legs felt weak.

Slowly he entered the house.

Things were out of place. Jackets had been flung off the pegs in the hall. His fishing tackle had fallen from where he had laid it against the wall. He went into the living-room. He stood, open-mouthed, in the doorway. Things were not out of place in the living room; rather the room had been wrecked. Vandalised. The Latin temperament, he knew, was legendary. He possessed a streak of it in his own personality, but this was unreal. He wondered how she would react if he abused her, if this was how she reacted when confronted and asked to come clean.

Christ, that's all he had done, asked her to come clean, he had not suggested their relationship was over. He had not been seeing another woman. Far from either.

But, she does this. She didn't hang around, either; wrecked the house, packed her bags and left, all in the space of ninety minutes.

He went upstairs, dreading what he would find. At the top of the stairs he glanced into the table tennis

162

room and, by then, was not surprised to see the table had been heaved off the trestles and now lay flat on the floor.

He went to the bedroom. Wrecked. Curtains torn down. Sheets ripped, duvet slashed, feathers everywhere.

On the bed were her cases. Half-packed. The remainder of her clothing hung in the wardrobe.

'Francesca!' Rossi yelled and heard his own voice echo in the vast empty house. 'Francesca!' he yelled again, beginning to dash from room to room. 'For Christ's sake, what's happened?'

It was a soft noise that stopped him. A soft noise amid all the destruction. A whimpering.

It came from the bathroom.

Chapter 7

SHE SAT ON THE SOFA, with her legs curled under her, sipping the brandy. Outside, dawn was breaking, cold and grey.

Occasionally her eyes flickered. Occasionally it seemed that she registered some sound, some movement. Once, her mouth formed the beginning of a smile. She was coming out of shock.

She sipped the brandy. He sat opposite her in an armchair, stubble on his chin, crumpled clothes, drinking coffee as indeed he had been drinking coffee to keep himself awake all night. Now at 7.30 a.m., and awash with the liquid, he couldn't drink what remained in the mug and placed it down beside the chair. In the half-light, the wreckage and devastation of the vandalised room formed strange shapes. Rossi shivered slightly.

He had found her crumpled, whimpering in the sunken bath, unhurt but frightened and in a state of deep shock. She had been easy to handle and Rossi had been able to ease her out of the bathroom and, in doing so, only then did he notice the unmistakeable small arms fire damage to the bathroom door. She had taken refuge in the bathroom, locked herself in and somebody, once in the house, his house, had shot the lock off the door presumably in order to then shoot her. Rossi had, with all gentleness, taken her downstairs into the living-room, thrown a blanket around her shoulders and waited until she recovered. About one hour before dawn, he gave her a generous measure of brandy. She began to sip it slowly, not requiring encouragement.

Let her take her time, Dominic. Let her move at her own pace.

A milk float whirred past the house. The paper boy in Doc Marten's crunched up the gravel drive and clattered the morning paper through the letter-box and crunched away again. Her eyes flickered at the sounds and her head turned slightly to follow them.

'Somebody is trying to kill me,' she said suddenly in a trembling voice. 'If you hadn't come back, I'd be dead now.'

Rossi said nothing, he didn't want to press her, but nodded his head, slightly, telling her that he had heard her, that she was free to continue speaking, that she was not distressing him or upsetting him.

She sipped the brandy. 'I didn't believe it at first. I was so . . . so stupid . . . he's had them all killed, you see. All the people who were in the cell; his cell.'

'Cell?' Rossi probed gently. The word 'cell' had

implications and a possible meaning that he didn't like at all. He felt a certain hollowness in his stomach. 'What cell is that, Francesca?'

She paused, sipped the brandy and then said, 'Our cell, he was our leader; Pietro was our leader. I think that he became a priest; in fact I know that he became a priest and was given a parish in the mountains; a village called Cocullo. I don't know if he is still a priest; probably not, if he is orchestrating the murder of all his old comrades.'

'Leader of what, Francesca?' Rossi sat forward in the chair. 'Look at me, look, now just tell me; tell me, what the hell are you involved in?'

Francesca returned his look and nodded. 'I think you have guessed,' she said.

'Tell me I'm wrong.'

She shook her head. 'On the boat, the other day, the pleasure boat on the Clyde, you pointed out the new Sheriff Court building. You told me about its design to withstand bomb blasts. . . .'

'No, it absorbs them,' said Rossi, 'it doesn't with-stand anything. But, go on.'

'You said something about terrorism being a real threat.'

'Yes, I remember.'

'And you saw a look in my eyes at the mention of the word "terrorism". There was a look in my eyes, just for a split second; when you talk to people and suddenly you strike a chord with them – it registers. . .'

'I remember.'

'I couldn't stop myself showing it. You saw it, I know you saw it.'

'Yes.' Rossi nodded. 'I did see it. I thought that you or your family might have been victims of some sort, either deliberate targets or victims of a bomb or sabotage.'

She shook her head. 'I was a member of *le Brigate Rosse*.'

'The Red Brigades . . .' Rossi's voice tailed off.

'*Si.* I mean, yes.' She sipped the drink, then took a stiff mouthful. 'I probably won't be able to enjoy this much longer.' She held the glass up in front of her eyes and studied the contents. 'Funny how you take things for granted all your life and then, when you look death in the face, and you realise that you don't have long to live, then little things become precious. I never knew how beautiful brandy was until now, until I realised that I may never have drunk even this, and this may be . . .'

'Cut it out!' Rossi snapped angrily. 'There'll be plenty of time for philosophising and plenty more booze. I want to know what you're involved in; I want to know who wrecked my home? Did he chase you around the building – is that why it's wrecked?'

She shook her head. 'He played a sort of cat and

mouse game, forced me to flee upstairs and then wrecked your house at leisure. Then, he came upstairs, found me in the bathroom, shot the lock . . . then you came . . .'

'I didn't notice anybody in my house, or leaving it.'

'I can't remember clearly. He may have left long before you arrived.'

'If that is the case, why didn't he kill you? He had the opportunity.'

'Then, he must be telling me that there is nowhere I can hide from him, nowhere in the world. It took him just forty-eight hours to trace me here. I think that's probably it, he probably wants to avoid killing me overseas . . .'

'That doesn't add up.' Rossi shook his head. 'It would be easier and neater to kill you outside Italy. If he's a professional.'

'Pietro is.'

'If he's a professional, then he wouldn't want to soil his own nest.'

'So, he's playing a cat and mouse game, a bigger cat and mouse game than he played in your house. He could be anywhere. Why would he want to hunt us down now? It's been nearly ten years. He must be planning to start again, with a new cell and we know too much. He's frightened that we could inform, we could be turned by the police; we could be given immunity from prosecution if . . .'

'Get a grip on yourself!' Rossi stood; he stared incredulously at her. 'This has gone quite far enough.' He paused, collected himself. 'For Christ's sake, Francesca – the Red Brigades? Terrorism? You're not telling me that you're one of those bloody lunatics?'

'Dominic . . .' she reached out to him. He brushed her hand away.

'You know,' he said, shaking with anger, 'you know . . . I don't believe it . . . I don't . . . you . . . you came here to hide from them. So, it was all lies, all of it from beginning to end . . . you used me.'

'No.'

'When did it start? In Italy, I suppose? I suppose that that was what you were doing when you flaunted yourself on the beach in your bikini. You were looking to pull a mug, any clown would do, so long as he could help you save your hide. I thought that I knew about life, but I walked right into it, didn't I . . . I can't believe I didn't see it.'

'It wasn't like that.'

'I don't believe you. I don't. I think I'm more angry with myself. Christ, I should have seen it with a glass eye.'

Rossi stormed out of the room, marched down the hall, into the kitchen and banged his fist against the wall. Francesca followed him and stood in the doorway.

'Dominic,' she spoke softly, hesitantly. 'Dominic, if

I used you, it was because I used us; I used us, not you.'

'Really, that makes a whole lot of difference! I mean, that's all right, since you put it like that!'

'It was wrong of me.'

Rossi glared at her.

'Look, just stop looking at me as if I am some kind of monster . . . it was ten years ago . . . I'm just not the person I was then . . . Oh, God, Dominic. I should never have come here . . . I was just so frightened.'

Rossi responded with a sullen silence.

'I'll be out of here in ten minutes.' she said meekly. 'I just have to finish packing . . .'

Rossi nodded.

'I'll pay for the damage.'

Rossi didn't respond. Francesca turned away and left the kitchen. He didn't notice her leave, he was absorbed in his own thoughts. He felt a sense of betrayal compounding his sense of being used. Slowly the sound of Francesca packing her cases penetrated his consciousness. He left the kitchen and went upstairs. He stood at the entrance of the bedroom.

'What did you do in the Red Brigades?' he asked, after a silence.

'What difference does it make?' she said quietly. 'I was in the Brigades and that's it!' She paused. 'If you have to know, I was the housekeeper. I ran the safehouses for the ones . . .'

'For the ones who did the killing . . . well, now I suppose you *know* . . . sorry, that's unfair.'

'I know a bit about being killed. No. it's not unfair. The boot is on the other foot.'

'Where are you going?' he asked. 'Where can you go.'

'It doesn't matter. Does it matter?' She folded a skirt and laid it in the case. 'So long as I leave your house, surely that's all that matters.' She shut the case, picked up both of her bags and carried them to the door. Rossi put his arm across the door to bar her way. She caught her breath, and turned and looked into Rossi's eyes. He held her stare and eventually she fell against him, trembling with emotion. He put one arm around her and then, hesitantly, he put his other arm around her too.

* * *

In Cocullo, Father Pietro once again read the newspaper article which suggested a link between the murders in Rome. How right, he thought, how right the reporter was; how close to the truth. He crossed the room and took the photograph from the drawer. It had been dangerous of him to keep it, an unheard of risk, but he had kept it; the photograph of them all, the cell in the old days. He could no longer keep it, it was far too incriminating. He struck a match and set fire to the photograph. As he watched it burn, he kept

171

staring at Francesca's face and her image, out of the entire group, was the last to be consumed by the flames.

*   *   *

'It's ridiculous! Come on! Ridiculous, and I mean ridiculous.' Eleanor Goodchild stood facing Rossi, feet firmly planted on the floor, arms akimbo. Behind her, Rory Stuart-Frazer allowed himself to be distracted from spraying the plants and looked on with undisguised amusement.

It was the first time that Rossi had been in Eleanor Goodchild's flat – 'riverside penthouse', he thought, might be a better description. A top flat in the new development; balcony overlooking the Clyde, Kingston Bridge to the left, Kingston there just across the water, the *Daily Record* and Bilsland's Bakery at the back. She had decorated it tastefully, he thought, as he took it in with a sweep of his eyes – white upholstered three-piece suite, light brown carpet, glass coffee table, sliding doors onto the balcony which was covered with sloping glass, a print of abstract art above the sideboard, skylights in the ceiling.

'I just need twenty-four hours,' he said, 'I just need some place for her to stay. A couple of days at the very most. Just until I can get a few things sorted out.'

'So, put her in a hotel, moneybags!' she spoke slowly, with a hard edge to her voice.

'Won't do. Has to be a house.'

'Why? Anyway, what things?'

'Because she needs someone with her.'

'And what things? What's it all about?'

'That's the catch. No questions asked.'

Again she said that it was ridiculous.

'I know it's ridiculous.' said Rossi, calmly. 'I wouldn't ask you to do it unless it was really necessary.' He paused and said, 'Please!'

Eleanor Goodchild stamped angrily out of the room, then returned, walked to the glass doors which opened onto the balcony, sat in a chair, looked at the ceiling and then to her right and to her left. Then she said 'Yes.'

Rossi left the flat, went down the carpeted staircase to the front door, and walked to where Francesca sat waiting in his car. As Rossi approached the passenger door, Francesca wound down the window. He smiled, nodded.

'She said it's okay for you to stay for a couple of days.'

'Are you sure she doesn't mind?'

'Well, she minds a bit, but it's only for two days. Really, I think she's more surprised than anything. I caught her off guard. Come on, let's get you up there.'

'When will you come back?' she said, getting out of the car.

'Tomorrow, maybe in the evening.'

'Tomorrow evening,' she said. 'Thank you, Dominic. I can't tell you how much I appreciate . . .'

'Okay, okay . . .' he took her things from the boot of the car. 'That door, there – the one with the light on.'

In the event, he returned later that same evening.

He returned, and Eleanor Goodchild's expression of surprise at seeing him turned to an expression of concern.

'What's the matter, Dominic?' she asked.

'I need to talk to Francesca.' he said urgently.

'Certainly, she's on the balcony.'

Eleanor Goodchild led Rossi through her flat. Rory Stuart-Frazer nodded in surprise at Rossi's return. Francesca saw him and sat upright. She too had seen the concerned expression and the way he was looking at her. She knew that it could only mean bad news. He joined her on the balcony; he closed the glass doors behind him.

'When I got home,' he said, 'Just as I had arrived, the phone rang.'

'Italy?'

Rossi nodded. 'No name, just a message. Francesca, somebody has kidnapped your son. Somebody has kidnapped Sergio.'

When at length Francesca had composed herself, Rossi also added, 'The caller, he said that you would know what to do. What does that mean? Francesca, what do they want?'

'It is a summons. He wants me back. Back in Italy. Pietro wants to finish it where it all started. If he can't kill me, he will kill my child. What would any mother do?'

'That's what I guessed. So the man who came to my house, he really was playing a cat and mouse game with you.'

'I think so.'

'Pietro is well organised. He can't be in two places at once. He hadn't time to get from Glasgow to Rome between wrecking my home and kidnapping Sergio, so there's a cell at work. A new cell.'

Francesca nodded. 'And I am a piece of dead wood. An inconvenience. I shall return. I won't get a flight tonight, but tomorrow.'

'You're not going alone.'

Francesca's jaw dropped. She made to speak.

'No arguments; I'm coming with you.'

'Dominic, they're going to kill me. Haven't you heard what I've been telling you. They won't hesitate to kill you too. You are nothing to them. What do you think you can do?'

'I don't know. I just can't let you go back alone, that's it.'

She shook her head, smiled at him but there were tears in her eyes. 'I don't have long to live; you have everything to live for – your advocacy, your senior

175

partnership, your house . . .'

'Without you, I have nothing,' he said, holding her hand, holding her gaze. 'Nothing, it's all nothing without you. I don't care what you've done, my place is with you and nowhere else; and, if you are going to Italy, then I am going with you. That's final, no "ifs" or "ands" or "buts", nothing. No arguments at all. We leave tomorrow.'

*   *   *

'He's gone to Italy,' said Eleanor Goodchild.

'Bit sudden, wasn't it?' Flanagan ushered Goodchild into his office.

'Could say that.' Goodchild sat in front of Flanagan's desk and sniffed at the surroundings. 'One minute he'd booked his lady into my flat for two days and the next they were leaving to catch the first available flight to Italy. Something happened, some bad news. I don't know what. Anyway, the point is that he asked me to let you know that he won't be around for a day or two and he wants me to pick up where he left off.'

'I see. Good of him.' Flanagan nodded. 'Dare say that means that I have to put you in the picture.'

'That would be a good start, Mr Flanagan. You were one of Dominic's students when he did those seminars at the University, were you not?'

'I was.'

'It shows.' said Goodchild, 'the unmistakeable stamp of a maverick.'

'And pleased to be so.' said Flanagan. 'I can't tell you how proud I am to have done not one conveyancing, not once have I charged a substantial four-figure sum for what everybody knows is an afternoon's work.'

'It's not like that and you know it. If you want to buy a house with a public right of way going through the living-room, go get a cheap lawyer; if you want quality service, you pay, as in all things.'

'I think I'd better put you in the picture,' said Flanagan, sensing an unwinnable circular argument beginning to develop. He'd been that way before. 'Briefly, it is as follows. There are two young boys, Mickey Conner and Gerard MacLawrie; both have got track records for robbery, they are found with 18k in their possession, each claims he knows nothing about it and reckons it's all down to the other. Subsequently, both die. Gerard is a victim of a hit-and-run driver which, in the circumstances, is a bit suspicious. Mickey Conner's lifeless body is pulled from the Clyde with a wire ligature round his neck. Very suspicious.'

'Murder.'

'Right. So, we're into the big league. We suspect that the money might be the proceeds of a robbery, possibly from within the Chinese community.'

'Why?'

'The money, the eighteen thousand, hasn't been reported as being stolen, so Dominic thinks that it might be illegal gambling money from a Chinese gambling den.'

'It might be illegal money from anywhere; it doesn't necessarily point the finger at the Chinese.'

'It's a hypothesis.'

'You're not kidding.'

Flanagan let it ride. 'Dominic went to where one of the boys lived and found what appears to be the plan of some premises.' Flanagan opened a drawer. He took out a sheet of paper and skimmed it across the top of the desk to where Goodchild sat. 'That's a photocopy of the plan found by Dominic. You can hang onto it for reference. We don't recognise the handwriting.'

'It's not admissible evidence anyway.'

'No, but it would point us in the right direction.'

'Doing this off your own bat as it were?' Goodchild folded the piece of paper and placed it in her handbag. 'I mean, where is the solicitor's interest? This is more like private sleuthing.'

'Dare say Dominic doesn't want to leave a job unfinished. His client was the hit-and-run victim.'

'I see.'

'There's a cop, Ballantyne, likes to be called Big Jim Ballantyne. Has a knack of popping up in all the wrong places and, wait till you hear this, goes for quiet drinks with known felons to the *Tuxedo Princess*.'

'Nobody goes for a quiet drink to the *Princess*.'

'You try telling that to Big Jim Ballantyne. Dominic bumped into him on the *Princess*, letting his hair down but he insisted that a felon was giving him information.'

'On the *Princess*! A likely story.'

'That's what Dominic thinks. Information from felons would be given in the snugs of wee bars in Partick, not on board the *Princess*, surrounded by the young and the beautiful. Dominic thinks that something's going down. Could be a connection, or there couldn't.'

'And that's it?'

'That's it. How about lunch? We could eat Chinese?'

'Why not.' She stood. 'You know, there's a point that occurs to me. The people who are behind the robbery, if they were Chinese, wouldn't go outside their own community and they wouldn't hire Gerard MacLawrie or Michael Conner for something like that. They were just kids.'

'Good point.' said Conner. 'Why them, indeed?'

*   *   *

He is probably the most fortunate of them. Carlo stood over the stupified body of Guilio, reeking of alcohol, surrounded by empty bottles, slumped on a small bed in a dark, airless room. The others, thought Carlo, had been conscious, they might have suffered a split second of realisation before the bullet, just a single bullet, crashed into their body. The woman, he smiled, he had tortured her for a full thirty minutes, left her a quivering, whimpering child, and had calmly left the house and returned to London by train. All in his own time. In doing so, he had told her that there was nowhere she could hide and Guilo, mercifully unaware of the executioner standing over him, had fulfilled his purpose.

As before, the gun leapt once in Carlo's hand, making a soft 'phutt' sound as it did so.

*　　　*　　　*

The restaurant was quiet, most tables were unoccupied. Eleanor Goodchild and Flanagan were shown to a table at the rear of the restaurant and a little isolated from the other tables; a table it seemed for prestige customers. Mr Wang and Mr Chen, who had earlier benefited from the shrewd advice given by Eleanor Goodchild on a proposed property purchase, stood by the table. They both wore a worried and a serious expression. Wang spoke.

'We have already told Mr Rossi and this gentleman, Mr . . .'

'Flanagan,' said Flanagan.

'Mr Flanagan. We have already told Mr Rossi and Mr Flanagan that we did not know anything about a robbery. We are a very law-abiding people. We don't want any trouble.'

'Yes.' Eleanor Goodchild leaned forward. 'We know that the Chinese community are a very law-abiding community. That's precisely why we need your help. Look, when Dominic and Tom here came to see you, they thought that the man who got the two boys to stage the robbery . . .'

'We said we did not know about it.' Wang interrupted suddenly, as if frightened.

'. . .they thought,' Goodchild continued,' that the man was from the Chinese community. But we think it was someone local, not Chinese. We're not trying to accuse anybody that you might know and we can't see why you should get a bad press. So, please, can you help us?'

Wang and Chen glanced at each other. Chen nodded.

'We told Mr Rossi the truth.' said Wang. 'We didn't know.'

'Since then,' Chen said, interrupting, 'we have asked – quietly, you understand.'

'And?' asked Goodchild.

'Mr Rossi was right, there was a robbery. Two young men in masks. They had guns.'

'Nobody knows who they were.' Wang added

quietly. 'And our people did not kill the two young men represented by Mr Rossi and Mr Flanagan. Our people did not run anyone down in the street, we didn't strangle anyone and throw their body in the Clyde.'

'I think we can guess who did,' said Flanagan. 'I don't mean his identity, not yet. I mean his place in the scheme of things.'

'Being?' asked Eleanor.

'Well, my money would be on the guy who set the whole thing up. Gerard and Mickey get caught quite by accident by the police, so Mr Big – well, he fills them in, or has them filled in before they talk. But we are nowhere near knowing who Mr Big is, are we?'

Eleanor Goodchild shook her head. 'That's life.' she said. 'One brick wall down and lo and behold, what lies ahead of you but yet another brick wall!'

'It's a hurdle race, all right,' Flanagan nodded. 'But, if you stop hurdling, you die. Shall we order?'

*   *   *

Signora Arcalli entered the high-ceilinged room. She was a woman with preoccupations, a hard-set face. There was a certain clumsiness and gaucheness about her movements as if she no longer wished to carry herself gracefully or perhaps felt that such skills no longer mattered. She glanced at Rossi, a brief sideways split second of eye contact, enough to register his presence without actually looking at him. She approached the drinks' tray and poured herself a stiff brandy. Rossi did not expect to be asked if he too would like a drink. He was not disappointed.

'I thought that you were prepared for the realities of life, Signora Arcalli,' he said, gently. 'Can I ask what happened?' Signora Arcalli didn't really answer the question, except perhaps by innuendo.

'Vincenzo's had quite bad concussion,' she sipped the brandy. 'I've just come back from the hospital.'

Rossi nodded. So, he reasoned, by implication, Sergio was snatched with force after his bodyguard was overpowered. Two men, three, so it was planned rather than a lone nut acting opportunistically when Vincenzo's attention was diverted. It tied in with the phone call.

'You shouldn't have let yourself get drawn into this, Mr Rossi.'

'Why not?' said Rossi.

Signora Arcalli turned to him and shrugged enquiringly.

'I didn't have much choice,' he said. 'They gave me the message for Francesca.' He paused and then added, 'From Pietro.'

Signora Arcalli stared at Rossi. Rossi held her stare. Matchpoint.

'Well, well,' said the woman, slowly relinquishing her stare, slowly allowing a thin, bitter smile to form on her lips. 'So, you have been learning all the family secrets. Not a lot left in the closet, is there.'

'I wouldn't know,' said Rossi. 'As in all things, like all of us, I know what I know, I don't know what I don't know.'

'Well,' she said, pouring herself another generous measure of brandy. 'I don't think that there's anything else for you to know, not in this case anyway. My daughter, your mistress . . .'

'My lover.'

'Your lover has a history that she is not proud of, that we – as a proud and ancient family – are deeply ashamed of. We keep the secret locked away just as, in the old days, family members who, for one reason or another might be social embarrassments, were locked away from the world. I assume the Arcallis did that to their lunatics and their monsters. I only assume that. I married into the family, but all families did that, back in history.' She drank deeply. She rocked a little on her feet. 'So terrorism is a twentieth-century monster that has to be locked away in the little room at the back of the house, the sort of room that only family members who have come of age, and trusted retainers, know about.'

'Is Vincenzo a trusted retainer?'

'Vincenzo is a mercenary. He is loyal, completely, unwaveringly loyal to one person; that is the person who is paying him. Vincenzo would guard Sergio with his life until somebody offered him more money to guard their child, in which case he would be gone without a word of notice or a backwards glance. No, Mr Rossi, Vincenzo does not know about Francesca's background and I'll thank you to ensure that if he does hear about it, he doesn't hear it from your lips.'

'You have my word.'

'And so, tell me, Mr Rossi, what would you have done if you had found that your daughter was involved in terrorism? Would you have handed her over to the police?' She paused. 'Thank God her father wasn't alive when she told us what she had done.'

'He might have got her out of it, instead of turning a blind eye. He was a powerful man. He could have negotiated reduced charges, maybe even total immunity in return for information.'

Signora Arcalli laughed sarcastically. 'She would not inform on her comrades and, as for her father pulling strings,' she shook her head, 'no, he would have argued that she had dug a hole for herself and it was up to her to get out of it herself. Only daughter or no only daughter. Only child. He was a hard man to Francesca when she was small. We argued about it. I said then and I still say that he did not allow her to love him. If Francesca had been allowed to love her father, then she would have not wished to make war on authority figures when she became a woman. She is a shrewd person, shrewd to the point of being calculating and I think that that is a survival mechanism which was born of emotional aridity in her childhood.'

Another generous measure of brandy went into her glass.

'Perhaps I am to blame. It is a woman who keeps a family together, but I was intimidated by my husband, I dared not do as much as I would have wanted.'

Francesca entered the room and stared at Signora Arcalli.

'I'm going to get him back,' she said angrily, bitterly. 'I'm going to get him back. I know where Pietro is. I'm going to get Sergio back.'

'You'd better do it quickly,' Signora Arcalli rounded on her daughter. 'Quickly! Quickly! Quickly! Now! Now! Now! I'm going to call the police, tell them the whole story, I can't live with this guilt any longer. If you can't come clean, I shall come clean for you.'

Francesca glared at Signora Arcalli, then spun on her heels and walked furiously out of the room, her footsteps echoing in the vastness.

'I mean it. She's the one who's caused the misery in this family, not me, not my husband. I'm not covering up for her; she set me and my husband against one another. It's not what I said a minute ago, if she would have accepted paternal authority, it would have been different; he did love her, maybe she wouldn't let him, not the other way round; she was so pig-headed as a girl and now my grandchild has been taken . . .' she fought back tears that welled up in her eyes. 'He's the one I care about and I meant it – this time I won't turn a blind eye.'

*   *   *

Cristaldi leaned forward as the phone on his desk rang.

'Cristaldi,' he said, picking up the receiver.

'She's back,' said the voice on the other end of the line. 'At the Villa Arcalli. She has someone with her.'

'Thank you.' said Cristaldi and replaced the receiver, slowly, thoughtfully.

Chapter 8

ROSSI INCHED HIS WAY to the end of the queue, passing his time as he did so by watching the traffic go past on the autostrada outside. When he raised his eyes, he was able to enjoy the mountains and forests in the distance. There was something real and immediate about his surroundings, something tangible, different somehow from the detached amusement with which he would observe a foreign country when on holiday. Now he wasn't on holiday, he had a purpose, a purpose as yet unclear, as yet undefined.

At the moment, all he could do was to follow the woman. She was set on one aim, one intention and, at the moment, all he could do was to go where she led, a bit like running behind the cart waiting for an opportunity to leap aboard and seize the reins. If not the brake.

And he was doing this because the alternative was turning his back on her and returning to Glasgow. Impossible.

He reached the end of the queue, paid the cashier for the coffee and sandwiches. He noticed the cashier avoided the eyes of the customers. She was dark even for an Italian, she was very dark and hirsute, manfully so, and severely obese. Rossi assumed that she just couldn't take the inevitable sneers and smirks that she must frequently receive from customers. Rossi pondered on the cruelty of the mind that put such an unfortunate woman on public display. He reckoned she was about twenty years old. He hesitated before leaving the till; she glanced at him and he smiled at her warmly, approvingly and, in doing so, caught a glimpse of huge brown eyes, filled with the deepest of needs and suffering the most aching of all aching loneliness.

He walked across the café and laid the tray on the table. He took the coffee and sandwiches from the tray and they ate and drank in silence.

'Well?' Rossi broke the silence as a juggernaut thundered past, rattling the windows of the café.

'Well, what?' she asked, sullenly.

'Well, what's the grand plan? Two hours angry driving at breakneck speed, two hours out of Roma and not a word has passed between us.' She didn't respond.

'You're not going to tell me that two hours of thought haven't produced a plan of action.'

'Just leave it to me, will you, Dominic. You needn't have come. Thank you for doing so, but please don't push yourself in too far.'

'Well, it's been left to you for quite a while, you

can't just walk up to him . . .'

'Look,' she said angrily, loudly. At the next table, people turned to look at them, then looked away again. 'What do you know about it? It's between him and me and nobody else, and I know how to deal with it.'

'Just keep your voice down, will you.'

'Don't tell me to shut up.'

Heads turned. A tall, thin man sitting alone leered with sadistic pleasure at their difficulty. Others looked quickly away again, all having experienced a similar aspect of matrimonial bliss.

'So, tell me, how are you going to deal with it?'

'I don't know.'

'You said you did.'

'I'll know when I get there. I haven't enough information yet. I need more information before I can make a decision. Anyway, I'm not frightened. That's the main thing. While I'm not frightened, I am in control and he won't hurt me, not face to face, not in front of Sergio.'

'Not frightened!' Rossi's own voice raised higher than he had anticipated. 'You're scared stiff.'

'I'm not!'

'Yes, you are! And scared people do stupid things. Frightened animals act in desperation.'

'Oh, so I'm an animal now.'

'I didn't say that.'

Heads turned their way. The cashier dropped a customer's change, his change, as in many parts of Italy, being three boiled sweets.

'As good as.'

'And, anyway,' Rossi hissed, insistently, 'why not, why won't Pietro hurt you just because Sergio's there? So, what's the big influence that Sergio can pull.'

'Work it out for yourself, pea brain!' She shouted, thumping the table. 'You know how old Sergio is.'

'Ten. So what? What the hell's his age got to do with it?'

'Because,' Francesca dropped her voice to a whisper, 'because of what I told you that I was involved in ten years ago. Were you born stupid or did you just work very hard to achieve that state of grace? Pietro's his father!' She stood, her chair fell backwards and clattered on the floor. She turned on her heel and walked out of the café.

Rossi leaned back in his chair, devastated. Then he became aware of a heavy silence in the room, of all heads turned his way. He shrugged his shoulders and raised his arms.

'Hey,' he said in fluent Italian, addressing the room, 'it's our first wedding anniversary, so what the hell.'

Two people applauded him.

In the car, Rossi said, 'I told them we were married. I said it was our first anniversary.'

Francesca smiled. 'I hope I never have to go in there again. But, I repeat, I'm sorry I lost my temper.'

'It's all right, I won't make a Federal case out of it. But why didn't you tell me earlier – I mean about Pietro being Sergio's father?' Rossi looked ahead out of the windscreen at the mountains in the distance.

'I have no real excuse. Will you believe me when I say that I wasn't deliberately keeping you in the dark. Perhaps I thought that you had had quite enough unpleasant surprises.'

'Well, for future reference, perhaps you'll remember that we are supposed to be a partnership. Nasty surprises or no nasty surprises.'

'All right, I apologise.'

'Do we have far to go now?'

'No, not far. We'll be turning off the *autostrada* soon. It's up in the mountains ahead.'

'What do you say the place is called?'

'Cocullo,' she said, pronouncing it 'Ko-koo-low'. 'Some people have summer homes there, but it's very small with a wintertime population of less than fifty.'

'Really.' Rossi raised his eyebrows.

'It's a medieval village, on the top of a mountain, but with higher peaks around it. It was occupied by the Germans in the war because there was partisan activity in the mountains. Even today there are bandits in the hills.'

'So I heard.'

'There's a place where we can stay tonight. Just a few miles from the village.' She glanced at Rossi and smiled. He returned her smile.

'I don't know about you, but I'm tired. But not that tired.'

*   *   *

In an office within a substantial and solid building in Rome, Cristaldi studied a map which he had spread over his desk.

'Good,' he said, 'Good.'

'Sir?' His assistant glanced at Cristaldi.

'Well, she's going somewhere, she is leading us to the man Pietro, the leader. I'll bet one year's salary that that is where she is going. Put everybody on standby, Alfonso, we are coming up to the last lap.'

'Yes, sir.'

'Tell Carlo. . . no don't! I shall tell Carlo myself. His special talents are going to be needed again tomorrow or the day after that.'

'Yes, sir. Should I also inform the Minister?'

'Of course,' said Cristaldi, once again studying the map. 'Afterwards.'

*   *   *

'I still don't think we should do it.' Flanagan said, quietly.

'Well, it's too late now.' Eleanor Goodchild

avoided eye contact with Flanagan. 'Look, I know that you're unhappy about it, but the law is the law and, anyway, I've told him that we have it so like I said, it's too late.'

'So long as my protest is noted.'

'It is.'

Ballantyne looked at them from his table in the restaurant of the *Tuxedo Princess*, finishing his meal at leisure. Eleanor Goodchild glanced around her; white satin table-cloths, chairs upholstered in pink, matching carpet, pillars in the room supporting the deck above, a bar, with gold columns behind the spirit rack. Outside, she could see the uprights of the Kingston Bridge. Music played softly.

Ballantyne signed the bill for his meal and handed it to the waiter. He finished his coffee, left the table and walked over to where Goodchild and Flanagan sat.

'Let's have the evidence, then?' he said, smiling smugly.

Goodchild opened her handbag. 'It's not evidence as such,' she said, handing him the sheet of paper that Rossi had found hidden in the caravan at Govan, 'it's just information; help to point the boys in blue in the right direction.'

'Very public-spirited of you. Quite a different attitude from your senior partner, the notorious Mr Rossi.'

'He happens to be a friend of mine,' Flanagan eyed Ballantyne coldly.

'That's your problem,' said Ballantyne. 'Me, I'm just happy that he's no friend of mine.'

'I'm sure he'll be delighted to hear that.'

'I don't think that this is getting us anywhere,' Goodchild snapped at both men, then, addressing Ballantyne, she said, 'As you see, it's a map of some premises, not identified; the handwriting is distinct, so that may help your quest.'

Ballantyne studied the drawing. 'Where was it found?'

'In the caravan where Mickey Conner lived up to his death.'

'Which was where?' Ballantyne asked.

'I don't know,' said Goodchild.

'You?' Ballantyne glared at Flanagan.

'Similarly,' said Flanagan. 'I don't know.'

'Have to ask Mr Rossi, then, won't I?'

'Have to wait until he gets home, won't you?' said Flanagan.

'Where is he?'

'Out of town,' Flanagan replied, not giving anything away.

'He's in Italy.' Goodchild said, defusing the tension. 'He's had to go there for a few days. Personal business. I don't know any details.'

'And you don't know when he'll be back?'

Goodchild shook her head.

'I don't either.' Flanagan said, coldly. 'But, the difference between me and this lady is that if I knew, I still wouldn't tell you.'

'Well, I'll just have to wait until Mr Rossi returns from his travels.' Flanagan folded the paper and put it in his jacket pocket. 'Still, thank you for this. You have been two busy little bees, haven't you?'

'What are you going to do?' Eleanor Goodchild asked.

'I'm going to do my job. See you, Ms Goodchild. I'll never forget what you did to me that day in court, but,' he tapped his jacket where he had pocketed the piece of paper, 'I'm pleased that we can work together if we try.'

'Like you, I was just doing my job,' said Goodchild. 'You did leave yourself open.'

'I'll just watch my back in future.' Ballantyne turned to leave. 'Especially when you're around.' He sauntered out of the restaurant.

Flanagan and Goodchild watched him leave and then turned to face each other.

'Smug bastard,' said Flanagan.

'I don't like him anymore than you do but we couldn't keep that information from the law. Besides, could you think of anything better to do?'

'I'm still not happy. Come on, let's go.'

They stood and left the restaurant area, walking

out of the foyer, under the canopy and down the green-painted metal gangplank.

'I felt a bit under-dressed.' Goodchild said as they stepped onto the gangplank. 'Next time I come here, I must remember my ankle chain and white stilettos.'

'Oh, don't be. . .'

'Excuse me! Sir! Madam!'

Flanagan and Goodchild turned around. The waiter who had served Ballantyne was calling after them.

'We must have forgotten something,' Flanagan walked up to meet the waiter, who ran down the gangplank towards them.

'Has Inspector Ballantyne gone?' asked the waiter.

Flanagan nodded. 'Yes, he left just a minute before we did. Why?'

'He forgot to take a copy of his bill – for his receipt. Always makes a fuss about it so he does. Do you work with him? Can you give it to him?'

'It's not what I'd like to give him,' said Flanagan, taking the paper from the waiter.

'Oh, give it to me.' Goodchild snatched the paper from Flanagan's hand. 'We'll have to go in tomorrow and make statements and if you have it, you'll just start exchanging blows with each other.' She put the bill into her handbag. The waiter returned to the restaurant.

Flanagan and Goodchild left the *Tuxedo Princess*. It

was night. Traffic hummed on the Kingston Bridge.

'See you around,' said Goodchild. 'I'll tell Dominic that you did well.'

'Thanks.' replied Flanagan, with a note of irony in his voice. 'Do you want a lift home.'

'I live about three hundred yards away, down by the riverside.'

'Just like the song.'

'That's it. Thanks anyway.'

Goodchild walked home, strolling under Kingston Bridge. She reached the flats, unlocked the street door and entered the carpeted common stairway. She went up to her flat and let herself in. She went straight upstairs to the living-room, dropping her bag onto the sofa. Walking across the room she picked up a plant spray and sprayed the plant which stood on a table in the corner. She returned to the sofa and sank onto it, stretching her legs as she did so and pinching the bridge of her nose. It had been a long, long day.

And she had a headache.

She rummaged in her bag for the aspirins and, not finding them, emptied the contents of the bag onto the glass-topped coffee table. She opened the aspirin bottle, took two of the small pills and, as she did so, she glanced at the bill which the waiter had been so anxious to hand to Inspector Ballantyne.

Her heart missed a beat.

She stood, her legs shaking, and opened a drawer

in the sideboard. She took from it the photocopied drawing of the premises, the copy of the paper which Rossi had taken from the caravan in Govan. She sat once again on the sofa, steadying herself as she did so. She held the two pieces of paper, one in each hand.

There was no doubt about it. No doubt at all. The person who had labelled the drawing of the premises, had also signed the copy of the bill for the meal aboard the *Tuxedo Princess*.

She picked up the phone. Tom Flanagan's answering machine greeted her. Patiently, she waited for the message to end and, on hearing the single 'bleep', she spoke:

'Tom, it's Eleanor. I hope you haven't stopped off for a drink. Can you get over here as soon as you can? It's vital. It's flat twelve. I've got something to show you which you'll love. Gotcha, Mr Big, Gotcha.'

*   *   *

'It belongs to my mother's side of the family,' Francesca said, without embarrassment, as she showed Rossi into the villa at Castrovalva.

It was not unlike the Villa Arcalli in Rome. Huge, in a word. But older. Grander.

'Nobody living here?' Rossi stared in awe at the ceilings, the tapestries, two huge globes standing on the floor, the ancient oak furniture.

'Not at the moment.' Francesca replied. ' In fact,

it's hardly used now.' She paused. 'I came every summer when I was a child.'

She led Rossi through the vast echoing corridors, through rooms with furniture covered in dust sheets and into a kitchen with an ancient gas range. She turned a tap. Gas hissed. She shut the tap off again.

'Never know when the gas supply is on or off,' she smiled at Rossi. 'But, we're in luck.'

'Do you think so?'

'With regard to the gas,' she replied seriously, 'with regard to anything else, well, I suppose I've run out of luck.'

'We've both run out,' he said firmly. 'We're in this together.'

She reached out and touched his arm. 'Perhaps,' she said, after a pause, 'perhaps you could bring the groceries from the car. I'll wash some plates and cutlery. Tonight I shall prepare a fine meal.'

Rossi walked back through the vast house and out to where they had parked the car. He lifted groceries from the boot and then paused to look about him.

It was late evening. The air was still and cold, very chilly, and getting colder. In the foreground and middle distance, stunted olive trees filled the landscape; in the far distance, rugged mountains formed the skyline. A bell from an unseen church tolled across the landscape with a hollow, empty chime; closer to, an owl hooted. Rossi turned back to the house. The building was tall and imposing, but even in this light, he found it not at all intimidating. It had a homely quality about it. It was a warm building; there had been a happy home within its walls. A motorbike parked at the side of the house added, thought Rossi, as he returned to the open door, a touching note of the ordinary.

He returned to the kitchen. Francesca wasn't there. Water was being heated on the stove. He placed the groceries on the table and wandered the house, searching for her. He found her in an upstairs room. She had opened the shutters and was looking out at the mountains. She heard him come in. He knew she heard him, but she didn't turn.

'Your family really goes in for the simple life.' He joined her by the window. 'I've toured the house, looking for you. I could be forgiven for thinking that I was walking around a museum and art gallery.' She reached out and took his hand in hers.

'Money isn't everything. It's nicer to have than not to have, but it won't solve all your problems, and it may even cause a few.'

'Still, as you say, nicer to have than not to have.' They stood in silence, watching night fall over the mountains.

'You helped Pietro find his hideout,' said Rossi gently, breaking the silence. 'Didn't you?'

Francesca nodded. 'The police were closing in on

us after the Moro killing. You know, the Prime Minister. They were going crazy. There was one man, a senior police officer, a man called Cristaldi, he was very good and he hunted us like a man possessed; he had been hunting us for some time, but after the Moro killing, he hunted us with renewed vigour.' She paused and took a deep breath. 'Pietro ordered us to disband, go back to our ordinary lives. I used to tell Pietro about the time that I was a child, about here, this part of Italy, how remote it was, how quiet, where someone could disappear. He said that it would be perfect for his ordinary life.'

'So he came here? To this house?'

'We both came. Together. We stayed briefly, a few weeks. Then we separated. That was ten years ago. We have not seen each other since. But I heard that he took holy orders and became a priest and, by coincidence and nothing more, he was sent to a poor parish in the mountains, a place called Cocullo.'

'You told me.'

'It's not far from here. Less than an hour's drive. I think it's strange, that of all the parishes in Italy he could have been sent to, he should be sent to Cocullo, so close to the house in which he and I hid from Cristaldi.'

Later, after the meal, Rossi poured more wine into her glass and asked her how she had got involved with Pietro and the *Brigate Rosse*.

'Are you the prosecution?' she asked, 'or the defence?'

'Both, in a way.' he said. He paused for a moment and said, 'Let's say that you're in custody. I've been called in by your family. I've got to decide whether to take the case. Whether you have a good defence in law.' He smiled at her. 'Tell you a story. This guy's been arrested for robbing a bank and he calls me in. Says he's not guilty. I say the cops got him half a mile from the bank in a car with the money, a hood and a gun. he says somebody threw the money, the hood and the gun into the car when he stopped at traffic lights.'

'Go on.'

'Well, I go on to point out that his fingerprints are all over the money, the hood and the gun. He says he picked them up to see what they were, that's how they got his prints on them. I say, how come they found some of your hairs inside the hood?'

'And?'

'He looks straight back at me. "You're my lawyer," he says, "you explain that one."'

'So – explain to me,' she said. 'What's my defence in law?'

'Well, you were very young,' he said. 'Immature, full of naïve ideals. You didn't realise what you were getting into. By the time you did, it was too late.'

She shook her head. 'I'm sorry, Dominic. It wasn't

like that.' She paused. 'I knew exactly what I was doing. I wanted to destroy. I wanted to destroy things and people. You can't imagine how I felt. Some days, if they had let me near the button, I'd have fired all the missiles. All over the world.'

'I thought you ran the safehouses? Are you saying that it was more than that?'

A pause.

A nod of her head.

'Jesus,' Rossi hissed. 'Why? I can understand it when people have nothing, when they see all the wealth and power in the world, but you . . .'

'Why not!' she interrupted. 'I was just carrying on the family business.'

'What do you mean? You told me that your father was an industrialist.'

'He was. He was big on death. He was one of the biggest names in the Italian death industry. His factories made guns, bombs, all kinds of weapons. He sold them all over the world, to governments – people with power. That's where our wealth came from.' She paused. 'Do you know something, I didn't find out until after he died. I was fourteen years old and the daddy I was pining for turned out to be a man who went out to the office every day to deal in mass murder. When I was older, I went looking for the ones who wanted to strike back against the people my father dealt with. No naïve ideals. Just destruction.'

'Why aren't you still one of them? What happened?'

'I don't know. I realised that it was my dead father I wanted to destroy. I grew up. Sergio . . . it doesn't matter. No defence.' She looked bleakly at him. 'Still want to marry me, Dominic? Still love me?'

Slowly Rossi reached forward and touched her hand where it rested on the table.

'Yes, yes, indeed.' He paused. 'I'm here, aren't I?'

*   *   *

Eleanor Goodchild paced the floor of her living-room, occasionally glancing out of the window at the lights of Kingston as they winked at her from the far side of the ink-black river. More occasionally, she looked at her watch. Then her doorbell rang. She skipped downstairs to let Tom Flanagan in. She swung the door wide. Ballantyne stood there. Grinning.

'It's only me,' he said. 'You busy?'

'Yes.' Goodchild stammered. 'Yes, in fact I am; kind of.'

Ballantyne eased his way past her and stood in the entrance hall of her flat. 'Promise,' he said, still smiling, 'it won't take five minutes. Just a statement. I was in the area on other business and I thought I could kill two birds with one stone.'

'How did you find out where I lived?'

'Electoral register. We keep one at the police station.'

'Well, I'm expecting someone any minute actually.'

'Five minutes, honest, Miss Goodchild, not a minute longer . . .'

'I've never known a statement to take five minutes.'

But Ballantyne was in her flat and was going upstairs to the living-room. She shut the door behind him and followed him upstairs. They stood facing each other in the room.

'Please sit down,' she said. He sat and took out his notebook.

'Thanks, I'd really like to go over the method by which you acquired possession of the drawing you gave me earlier this evening.'

'I've already told you everything I know.'

'If you don't mind,' Ballantyne opened his notebook.

'Well, as I told you, Dominic found it in the caravan where Mickey Conner was living along with his mates. He showed it to Tom Flanagan and we showed it to you.'

'It's the only copy?'

'Yes,' she said quickly. 'At least, so far as I know.' Ballantyne smiled a thin, self-satisfied smile. 'As simple as that.'

'As simple as that,' said Goodchild, suddenly wondering whether she should have told Ballantyne that 200 copies had been run off, instead of denying the existence of any. She didn't know which lie held the greatest insurance.

'Your friend's late,' he said.

'Any minute now, I guess,' said Goodchild, glancing at her watch.

'Well, that's me. I'm off. I have that other bit of business to see to, just along the road; you know, the boat, the *Tuxedo Princess*. Forgot my receipt. No receipt means that no expenses are refunded. He likes the paperwork to be exact, does Mr McManus.'

'Well, if that's all, I'll see you out.'

Ballantyne remained seated. He folded his notebook and pocketed it. 'You failed the test, I'm afraid.'

'Test? I'm sorry, what test?'

'I've already been to the boat and the waiter told me that he gave my receipt to you. And since you said nothing about it, you must have put two and two together and realised that I am implicated in the deaths of Mickey Conner and Gerard MacLawrie, and in the robbery of eighteen thousand pounds which was to go towards paying off my gambling debts. It means that . . .'

Eleanor ran for the door.

Ballantyne leapt forward, springing like a greyhound from a trap. He grabbed Goodchild by the arm and slapped her face. He fell on her, pushing her back onto the sofa, both hands round her neck.

'Good job you're short of folk through the wall in this place,' he said, squeezing his hands round her throat.

Goodchild kicked, scratched, pummelled him with her fists. But she was small. He was big. Very big. He began playing with her, slightly loosening his grip, then tightening it again.

'Pity,' he said, mocking sadness. 'Pity the boys got caught with the money. If they hadn't, then this wouldn't have happened. Shame, eh?'

Goodchild kicked him. She scratched his face. She felt her head exploding as his grip tightened.

'Tell you something else, hen. Forty-three per cent of all fatalities occur in the home. So now,' he said, forcing her off the sofa, 'you and I are going to the kitchen – a very dangerous place.'

She hammered her fists on his chest, then she looked about her, searching for a weapon, a knife, a heavy ashtray . . ..

The plant spray.

It was in reach. She grabbed. Directed it as his eyes and squeezed and kept squeezing.

'You bitch!' Ballantyne spat the words. He shook his head. He grunted. He took one hand from her throat and squeezed his eyes. Then he released the other hand.

Goodchild sprayed his eyes again. And the inside of his mouth.

He began to choke.

Goodchild picked up a plant pot. She brought it down on his head.

No effect.

She did it again. The pot shattered.

She picked up a paperweight.

She hit him.

She hit him again.

He still stood gasping, choking, occasionally lurching for her, but mostly using his hands to ease the burning in his eyes.

Goodchild sidestepped him and hit him again. On the head. As hard as she could.

His knees buckled.

She hit him again.

He went down.

She sank backwards, onto the sofa, just as her doorbell rang. She forced herself to stand up, negotiated the stairs with legs that felt like jelly. She reached the front door and opened it. Tom Flanagan looked at her with worried curiosity.

'You missed the fun,' she said, falling back against the wall. 'Your Mr Big is upstairs. He tried to kill me.' Flanagan entered the flat and ran upstairs. He displayed a mixture of emotions as he stood over

Ballantyne's body; aghast, delighted, surprised.

'It was his handwriting on the receipt that did it,' said Goodchild, sitting down. 'His handwriting was the same as the handwriting on the plan of the building. He knew that I had the receipt and he knew that I knew about him. He was going to kill me.' She buried her head in her hands and burst into tears.

Flanagan stepped over Ballantyne's body and picked up the phone. 'This is one call to Inspector McManus that I'm going to love,' he said, pressing the buttons.

Chapter 9

AND LATER, after the meal, later when he had suddenly, but gently, risen from the table and taken her by the hand and led her through the magnificent, empty house, up the wide staircase to the bedroom. Later, after they had tugged at each other's clothing, tearing at stubborn buttons and zip fasteners, and had fallen on the bed . . . later still, when they lay quietly under the single sheet, Rossi said:

'Francesca, you must know that I love you. I love you so very much.'

She reached for him, found his arm, ran her hand down to his and squeezed it tightly.

Later still, Francesca eased herself from the bed and dressed quickly and silently. She crossed to the window, opened the shutters and looked out. She saw the first glimmer of dawn driving wedge-like between the mountains and the night sky.

It was the dawn of her last day.

She closed the shutters and went over to where she had left her suitcase on the floor beside the old oaken wardrobe. She opened it slowly and quietly and fumbled inside until she found what neither her mother nor Rossi knew she had taken from the Villa Arcalli in Rome and which, unknown to Rossi, had travelled with them. It had come from Vincenzo's room, slipped easily away. His gun.

She closed the case and stood looking down at the still sleeping Rossi. She spoke softly.

'I love you, Dominic. You may not believe me but someday I'll prove it to you. I may not have done so at first, but I do now. I really do. You are a good man, a wonderful, wonderful person.'

She left the room quietly, closing the door behind her.

Rossi's sleep was penetrated by the sound of a car being started somewhere outside the house, just below the window. He opened his eyes and, in his half-sleep, he became aware that he was alone in the bed. He shook himself awake, flung the sheets away from him and walked rapidly across the bedroom floor to the window. He opened the shutters in time to see their car, the car in which he and Francesca had travelled from Rome, disappearing down the long tree-lined driveway.

Beyond, dawn rose brilliantly over the mountains.

Rossi pulled on his clothing and ran out of the room. He took the stairs to the ground floor two at a time and burst out of the front door of the house. The low sun glared and forced him to shield his eyes. Frantically he looked around, no such thing as a second car parked conveniently with the keys in the ignition, and a warm engine. Even a horse and trap would be . . . .

The motorbike.

He remembered the motorbike, the bike he'd seen leaning on its stand at the side of the house yesterday evening when he'd fetched the vegetables from the car. He ran to it, pulled it upright and sat astride it.

He kicked the starter down.

Nothing.

He kicked it again.

Nothing.

He kicked it again.

Nothing.

He kicked it again. Harder.

It spluttered into life and died.

He checked the tank. Half full.

He kicked the starter down.

The machine roared into life.

He worked the throttle, breathing strength into the life of the engine before asking it to take the load from the transmission. He engaged first gear and let in the clutch and drove unsteadily down the drive.

Francesca had driven her car through a puddle near the bottom of the drive. Her wet tyres left a clear indication of a right turn. Rossi followed her.

He drove down a narrow pasty road which wound and undulated between rocky fields of stunted olive

213

trees, of stone-built cottages, with tethered dogs which barked as he passed. Rossi scanned the road ahead, hoping for a glimpse of Francesca's car, but there was never an uninterrupted view of more than 300 yards. He drove on as fast as was safe. One kilometre. Two, three.

He came to a crossroads. No helpful tracks to help him here. He scanned the signpost. 'Cocullo' said one wooden arm pointing left, '15 kilometres.' Rossi wrenched the bike round.

He rode on, gathering speed, throwing the bike into corners. The landscape remained the same, low stunted olive trees, rocky soil, farmhouses squatting in the folds of the hills. The farmhouses seemed to be getting more frequent in number. He passed a small church and a roadside shrine. He was approaching a village. Then he saw the cluster of buildings ahead. A small tightly-packed village, with the houses surrounding the church.

The road was blocked. A *carabinieri* vehicle was slewed across the road. Two *carabinieri* stood by it, relaxed, helmets off, smoking cigarettes. Rossi slowed to a stop. They nodded at him as he approached.

'I want to go on,' he said. 'I have to go into the village.'

'It's not possible, said one of them, the older of the two. 'Manoeuvres, you know, exercises. The road has been closed since last night. Perhaps it will be open in an hour or two.'

Rossi shook his head slowly, slowly realising the implications, fighting disbelief. 'No,' he said, 'I am following a car, a woman, not ten minutes in front of me.'

'Signor,' said the *carabiniere*, 'there has been no vehicle past this spot for three or four hours, since we have been on duty and this road-block has been here for ten hours before that.'

Rossi turned the bike and drove away. No point in arguing. He drove around the first corner from the road block and coasted the bike to a halt. He left the machine at the side of the road, scrambled over a low wall and into the fields. He kept low, moving from tree to tree, moving towards the village.

*　　　*　　　*

Francesca drove up to the church. She parked the car in front of the building and looked about her as she got out. The village was still, silent, not very unusual for the time of day, but just a little unusual, she thought, a little odd not to see another living soul. There was normally somebody up and about at this time. She glanced at her watch, 7.00 a.m. Yes, normally she could expect to see someone. And so quiet. Still and so very quiet.

It was as if the village was brooding.

Or waiting.

She walked up the steps of the church and entered the building, taking Vincenzo's gun from her bag as she opened the door. She thought that Pietro, Father Pietro, might be in the church or still asleep in the presbytery. He would be in one place or the other.

He was kneeling at the altar.

She hesitated, looking down the aisle of the small church, dim in the early morning light. It was the first time that she had seen him for ten years. It was Pietro, the same strong back and broad shoulders, the same full head of black hair.

She approached him. Silently.

Pietro genuflected and then, sensing someone behind him, he turned.

She saw the shock register in his eyes, his mouth opened. It was not the reaction she had expected. Her finger hesitated as it began to curl on the trigger.

'Father Pietro,' she said. 'So, it is true. You have exchanged one calling for another.'

'Francesca.' Pietro gasped. 'What are you doing here? Are you mad? Crazy?'

'I think that you are the crazy one. I'm here to stop the killings. One more death and then they stop.'

'Me? Francesca, I have had nothing to do with them. Believe me. I have read of them in the newspapers, but other than that, I know nothing about them, nothing at all.'

*   *   *

Rossi reached the edge of the village and walked quietly down a cobbled street between the tall, three-storey houses. At the bottom of the street he hesitated, inched up to the corner and peered round it. No sign of life. No movement. No sound. Strange.

Even stranger was the military lorry parked and unattended. He waited for a few seconds. Catching his breath, he then walked on, warily.

*   *   *

'What about Sergio?' asked Francesca, holding the gun steadily, pointing it unwaveringly at Pietro's chest. 'Where is he?'

'Sergio?' Pietro repeated. 'What about him?'

'You know very well what about him. You took your own son – to lure me here, to kill me, and you sent a henchman to Glasgow to tell me that there was nowhere I could hide.'

'To Glasgow!' the priest gasped. 'Have you taken leave of your senses?' He stepped forward with two confident strides and, with a fluid sweeping motion, gently but firmly took the gun from her hand. She relinquished it without a struggle.

'Why would I want to do that?' Pietro checked the gun. 'It's loaded all right,' he said. 'These bullets could penetrate steel, but you hadn't got the safety catch off.' He turned the small lever at the side of the weapon and then handed it back to her. 'There, now you can shoot me if you want to, but perhaps you now believe me. If you were right, I wouldn't have returned the gun.'

'You don't have to tell me that.'

'Who have you brought here with you, Francesca?'

'No one. I came alone.' She shook her head. 'A friend. But he's at Castrovalva. You remember the house, those days we spent. . . .'

'I mean who has followed you, Francesca?'

She shook her head slowly. 'Oh, no, no, what have I done . . . what have I done? . . . not Cristaldi . . . not after all these years. . . .'

'We had better go. There's a place you can stay. Quickly! Put the gun away.'

*   *   *

It was bewildering. It had a strange dream-like quality, even later, remembering it, going over it when sitting alone at home, Rossi couldn't recall the exact sequence of events.

They came from nowhere. That was the first impression. One minute the streets had been empty, then they had been full of soldiers, armed, in full combat gear, pouring out of doorways, into the streets, converging on the church.

A man in civilian dress sat in the rear of a jeep talking on a hand-held radio.

The church door opened.

Francesca and a priest appeared.

Rossi shouted. He shouted that it was a trap, he heard himself shouting, but his voice seemed distant, remote.

Soldiers turned and looked at him. They levelled their rifles at him.

Francesca heard him. She turned to him and she came down the steps.

She came down the steps. She came down the steps.

Go back you fool, but she came forward.

Rossi shouted to the soldiers, 'Don't fire, don't fire!'

Francesca realised what was happening, she looked frightened, the soldiers advancing, Rossi shouting. . . .

She took the gun from her bag.

Rossi ran forward.

The priest raised his hands.

Francesca threw the gun down. It clattered on the steps.

Rossi ran forward. Good girl, sensible girl. He stood, panting, between Francesca, the priest and the soldiers. 'Don't shoot!' he said. 'Don't shoot!'

But the silence was rent by the chatter of a machine-gun from the side.

Rossi turned. Then it was slow motion. The priest

and Francesca fell slowly, a red haze coming from their bodies.

Their eyes met. Briefly. A split second. But it was enough. As she fell, her eyes met Rossi's and his eyes met hers.

Rossi turned to his right. A *carabiniere* removed his helmet and wiped his brow with his sleeve, holding the machine-gun at his side with his other hand. He looked at Rossi. The man's face was expressionless; then he called to Rossi.

'It was I, signor,' he said. 'I am in your house. It was not good but I am told to do it.' Then he turned and walked away.

More *carabinieri* ran forward and picked up the bodies of Francesca and Father Pietro, as a vehicle roared up to the steps. Rossi stood numbly as the bodies were bundled into the rear of the vehicle, looking more like blood-soaked bundles of clothing than the human beings they had been just a moment earlier. He staggered into the church and slumped into a pew. He rested his head on his forearm and then looked up. The man he had seen in the rear of the jeep, the man in civilian clothing, stood some distance away.

'A trap,' said Rossi, bitterly. 'Your trap. Right from the very beginning.'

'Yes,' said the man, the man called Cristaldi.

'You could have taken them alive. They were surrendering.'

'Neater this way,' said Cristaldi.

'Who are you? The army?'

'Mostly police,' said Cristaldi. 'The Anti-Terrorist Squad.'

'And what was the point of that needless bloodshed on the steps of a holy place?'

'We have been hunting Pietro for years. We were getting nowhere. I thought that if I, if we, eliminated the cell members we knew, then it would seem that Pietro was doing it and the woman Arcalli. . .'

'Signora Arcalli to you.'

'The terrorist Arcalli to you, Mr Rossi. . .. Then she would lead us to Pietro. And that is what happened. There were a few unexpected complications along the way; mostly you, but that's life.'

'That's murder!'

'The woman was armed.'

'Stop it!' Rossi shouted. His voice echoed in the church. 'She's got a name. Use it! And she threw her gun away.'

Cristaldi shrugged. 'Perhaps if you hadn't got in the way, I might have seen that.'

'Don't pull that stunt. You could see very well and so could that animal who shot them.'

'Carlo. Yes, he's very good.'

'What,' said Rossi softly, after a pause, 'what about the child? Sergio? Where is he?'

'Right now,' Cristaldi glanced at his watch. 'Home with his grandmother, I expect. Which is my advice to you Mr Rossi. You're a good man, you don't want to get caught up in this. Go home!'

'Not before I tell every newspaper and every television camera I can find what I saw out there.' Rossi stood angrily, squaring up to Cristaldi.

'I wouldn't advise it. We can make things difficult for you,' replied Cristaldi calmly. 'Remember, you have been in league with a known terrorist who was armed and who is proven dangerous. Italian justice is a slow-moving game, Mr Rossi. You will be in prison for years before you even come to trial. Go home!'

'You bastard!'

'Perhaps.' Cristaldi turned and walked towards the door and then turned back and approached Rossi. 'I should like to show you something.' He took a photograph from his wallet and handed it to Rossi.

'Lovely children,' he said. 'Beautiful wife.'

Rossi took the photograph and looked at it.

'My children,' said Cristaldi. 'My wife. At least they were, until a bomb planted by your lady friend and her comrades blew up the car in which they were travelling. She was taking them to school. Can you imagine that, Mr Rossi. It wasn't as though I was the

222

intended target, because we had separate cars, myself and my wife.'

'I didn't know,' said Rossi, meekly. 'I just didn't know.'

'It's the way of things in Italy. If the Mafia wishes to mete out vengeance, they will not shoot their enemy, they will shoot his family. I was getting close to them; they knew it and so they killed my wife and children. They tried to scare me off, but it only stiffened my resolve. I had to wait ten years to eat but I have enjoyed every morsel.'

'What do you mean?' Rossi handed the photograph back to Cristaldi.

'A private sentiment,' Cristaldi looked at the photograph before placing it back in his wallet. 'Something an old woman in black said to me, many years ago.'

'And what about their child. You've just made the terrorist leader of the next generation.'

'I'll be around,' said Cristaldi. 'And, I'll be waiting for him.'

Cristaldi left the church, walking slowly, his footsteps echoing under the vaulted ceiling. 'Just go home, Mr Rossi!' he said, when he reached the door. 'Go home and put it all behind you.'

Rossi walked out of the church. Outside, all military and *carabinieri* presence had vanished and the villagers were approaching the scene of the carnage in twos and threes. As Rossi appeared on the steps of the church, the villagers looked at him curiously; he was, after all, a player in the tragedy that had been visited upon their village.

Rossi stood over the bloodstains on the church steps and made the sign of the cross.

It was all he felt that was left for him to do.